SOLDIER

VICTORY AT NORMANDY

DOGS

READ ALL THE

SOLDIER DOGS

BOOKS!

SOLDIER
VICTORY AT NORMANDY
DOGS

MARCUS SUTTER

ILLUSTRATIONS BY ANDIE TONG

HARPER FESTIVAL

An Imprint of HarperCollinsPublishers

HarperFestival is an imprint of HarperCollins Publishers.

Soldier Dogs #4: Victory at Normandy
Copyright © 2019 by HarperCollins Publishers
Flag artwork on page iii and photo on page v, used under license from Shutterstock.com
www.harpercollinschildrens.com
Library of Congress Control Number: 2018968508
ISBN 978-0-06-284409-5
Typography by Rick Farley
19 20 21 22 23   PC/LSCH   10 9 8 7 6 5 4 3
❖
First Edition

To all the soldiers who lost their lives taking back France.

You are gone, but never forgotten.

PROLOGUE

A bolt of lightning arced through the clouds like the crooked fingers of an electric skeleton. Thunder rippled across the sky.

But when the storm died down, a different kind of thunder and lightning continued. The sounds came in deep thuds and rattling bursts, accompanied by shrieking whistles and angry whirrs. The light flickered both on the ground and in the air. And in those flashes, shapes could be seen—planes flying low, fortresses on the beach, men hanging from parachutes that billowed over them like mushroom caps.

The storm of battle.

The first rumblings of what would be one of the longest days the world would ever know.

As Henri and Elle ran for their lives, every second felt like a hundred years. Ace, the energetic Boston terrier separated from his American soldier handlers, bounded at their side. Behind them, merging with the rumbling of artillery, they could hear the throaty barking of larger dogs—Nazi Dobermans, running after them with teeth bared.

We have to outrun them, thought Henri. *If we don't, the war might be lost.*

The war had seen empires rise and cities fall. Germany had taken countless countries, but among the most important was France. Europe's jewel of art, culture, and free thought had been captured by Adolf Hitler's Nazi regime and his vicious, evil quest to conquer the world and make his word the only law.

The Allied nations standing against Hitler had been bombed and battered. Now they were ready to take back the world.

Now it was time for Operation Overlord—the plan to finally break the Nazis' iron grip on Europe.

In only a few hours, the beaches of Normandy, France, would be stormed by thousands of ships and submarines emerging from the English Channel. Countless Allied soldiers would rush the bunkers and fortresses along the countryside and attack the Nazi troops stationed there. They would take back Northern France and spread out into Europe, liberating people who had lost all hope.

If . . . Henri and his friends could outrun the dogs.

Henri's lungs burned as he sprinted down the road. Elle had begun to gasp with every breath. Even little Ace was slowing down. Behind them, he could hear the Nazi hound's barking getting louder and louder. Sweat ran in Henri's eyes as he put every last bit of strength he had into fleeing the enemy—but it was no use. The Doberman would reach them soon. If the Germans caught him, he was captured, at best. And Ace was certainly done for.

But it wasn't just them. It was the Resistance, who needed the plans tucked into Henri's coat pocket. It was Mother, who trusted Henri's courage but was no doubt worried sick about him. It was France, ruined by the Nazis, desperate for the strategies it needed to fight back and breathe free once more.

Henri wondered how he'd gotten here—running through the French countryside, carrying secret plans, fleeing the Nazis, his only friends in the world an orphaned country girl and an American dog who had literally fallen out of the sky. It made no sense. He shouldn't have offered to go on this mission. He should be with Mother, safe and sound. He shouldn't—

Elle's foot sank in the mud, and she went sprawling onto the ground.

Henri skidded to a halt and knelt next to her. He felt icy mud soak into his pants. Ace barked urgently at them, begging them to keep running. Henri tried to help Elle up, but it was no use— she was caught.

Henri turned his head and looked into the shadows. Ace stood there, facing the darkness with a growl. The Doberman approached fast, its eyes glittering in the flashes of light from the distant guns.

CHAPTER 1

OUTSIDE ROUEN, FRANCE
MONDAY, JUNE 5, 1944
12:43 P.M.

When Henri heard barking in the distance, he almost couldn't believe his ears. He'd thought he'd heard the sound of a dog before, but whenever he investigated it, he was always disappointed—it was just some chirping bird or creaking wheel that only *sounded* like her barking.

He turned and stared down a Paris street. The cobblestones stretched off into a deep gray mist that draped over all of the city, turning the Eiffel Tower into a tall smudge of black.

Could it be?

A dark shape trotted out of the fog. It paused, barked again, and started running toward Henri. As it came nearer, the mist faded away, and Henri felt tears in his eyes.

Brigette! Somehow she had escaped the Nazis and found him! He couldn't believe it!

Henri ran with all his might, grinning ear to ear. After all this time, Brigette had found a way to come back to him . . .

No.

Henri skidded to a halt. The dog running toward him was far too big to be Brigette. In fact, it was getting bigger by the second, until it was monstrous. As the fog parted from around the oncoming shape, Henri saw that it wasn't his beloved dog at all. It was a huge black beast with glowing red eyes and a slobbering tongue that dangled out of a mouth.

"Go away!" cried Henri. But that only made the beast run faster. He turned around and ran, but the beast was bigger and faster than he was. As it closed in on him, the whole city around Henri seemed to fall apart. Windows exploded outward, throwing shards of glass into the street. Houses shook and crumbled in billows of stone, dust, and splinters. In the distance, the Eiffel Tower was on fire and trailing an endless cloud of smoke. Giant cracks opened between the cobblestones at his feet, oozing black tar that gummed up his shoes and made him run even slower.

Henri looked over his shoulder just in time to see the beast leap into the air with its teeth bared . . .

"No!" he cried.

"Shh!"

Henri blinked, letting the image of the monster fade out of his mind. He rubbed the sleep out of his eyes as a warm hand wrapped around him and shook him lightly.

A dream. He'd fallen asleep, that was all. The beast, the city falling to pieces all around him . . . it was all just in his mind.

Not that the real world was much better.

Mother was at his side; it was her arm that held him close to her and rubbed warmth into his chilly bones. The men who sat crouched next to them, Monsieur Tardivat and Monsieur Anselle, shifted uncomfortably. Tardivat was distracted by what was happening up front, but Anselle glared at Henri with angry eyes staring out of his sunken, dirty face. His expression made Henri press closer to Mother—though that was difficult, given how cramped they already were.

The four of them huddled in a secret compartment in the back of a delivery truck. Pressed against Henri's right arm was a false back. On the other side, he knew, were crates of vegetables and bottled milk, scheduled for delivery to the German soldiers stationed in the fortresses along the Atlantic wall. The bed of the truck would appear perfectly ordinary to anyone who looked inside.

Especially—hopefully—to any Nazi soldiers searching for Jews or freedom fighters trying to flee Paris.

"Make sure that boy shuts up when we arrive at the checkpoint," hissed Monsieur Anselle, scowling at Henri. "I don't want my cover blown by some brat who can't keep his voice down—"

"Speak about my son that way again," said Mother in a calm tone, "and we will leave you by the side of the road."

Anselle's eyes bugged as Tardivat gave him a light slap on the arm and shook his head. Henri knew that neither of them were willing to anger Mother, especially since it was she who had arranged their transport to Fécamp in this truck. Without her connections in the British and French governments, they might not have gotten out of Paris at all.

And so far, the plan was working. Not that Henri was surprised—his mother, Linda Martin, was known for her brilliance and fearlessness when it came to outsmarting the Nazis. She had fought countless missions and evaded some of Germany's best spy-hunters. Among the French Resistance, her cleverness and speed had earned her a nickname, *le Renard Blanc*—the White Fox.

Mother patted Henri's shoulder and smiled down at him. "Bad dream?" she whispered.

Henri nodded. "It was about Brigette again."

Mother sighed. "I know you miss her, darling. But you must always remember that wherever she is, she still loves you."

Henri didn't respond. He wasn't stupid—Mother was trying to comfort him, but she was also trying to nicely tell him that Brigette was probably dead. Perhaps, he thought, it was even better that way. After the Nazis had taken her from him, Henri had worried that they would train her to be one of their attack dogs. Better Bri rest in peace than fight for the enemy.

Beneath them, the truck stopped, making their bodies rock. Henri felt it inch forward and stop again. From his left side, he heard loud voices speaking in German. Mother had taught him enough German words to get the basic idea: the soldier at the checkpoint wanted to know what the driver, Monsieur Barteau, had in the truck. Monsieur Barteau said vegetables and milk. The driver wanted to know if there were any extra supplies he could "borrow." Monsieur Barteau laughed and said there might be, but he wouldn't know until he came back through. The German snapped, and Monsieur Barteau finally said yes, fine, look in the back, but don't take too much.

"Is he mad?" whispered Monsieur Anselle, his

cheeks reddening. "Why would he send one of them back here?"

"Because people who get what they want don't look very hard for anything else," whispered Monsieur Tardivat.

"Silence," commanded Mother.

Henri sat still as a statue as Monsieur Barteau led the German around back and opened the rear of his truck. They listened to the heavy boots of the soldier move through the truck and stop—right outside the door to their secret compartment!

Fear shot through Henri, cold and sharp. He took a long, quiet breath through his nose and held it.

The clinking of bottles. A chuckle. "Ah, fresh milk," mumbled the soldier on the other side of the compartment. "My favorite!"

"Max, let's get going!" cried a voice outside. "All that milk is why you're so fat!"

"Yeah, well, who asked you," grumbled the soldier.

Henri exhaled slowly. They were safe, finally . . .

A crash made them all jump. Milk came spilling under the false back of the truck and into their compartment. Henri felt it soak into his pants, adding to the chill of fear that ran through his body. Monsieur Tardivat clamped a hand over his mouth and closed his eyes.

"Oof, I'm such a *tollpatsch* . . ." Henri didn't get that last word. He heard the German soldier begin picking up pieces of broken glass . . . and then the noise stopped.

"Wait . . ." said the German. "What . . . what's this—"

The door to their compartment jostled. The thin bolt on their side held.

Silence.

Maybe he'll go away, Henri thought.

A sharp yank. The bolt bent, and the door swung wide open.

CHAPTER 2

Henri felt his eyes hurt, they were so wide open. But by the looks of the German soldier, in the green uniform of a low-level infantryman and clutching a head of lettuce and a bottle of milk, his eyes hurt too.

At first, the Nazi stared at the huddled figures like he didn't understand what was happening . . . but when he saw Mother, a small smile crept over his face.

"*Guten Tag* . . . Madame Martin," he said, and reached for the pistol on his belt.

Henri gasped.

He knew who Mother was. She'd been dis-covered, finally, after all this time . . .

And yet when he glanced at Mother, all he saw was calm hatred in her eyes.

"Henri," said Mother calmly, "shins."

Henri knew the drill—pushing his back against Mother, he kicked out both his feet into the German soldier's legs. The Nazi cried out and stumbled to the floor. In an instant, Henri leaped over the fallen German and jumped out of the back of the truck, with Mother and her compan-ions hot on his heels.

Henri's eyes scanned the countryside and found a patch of woods at the top of the hill to his left.

"To the forest," he said. "We can hide there."

They ran as fast as they could. Behind him, Henri heard shouts in German, then the familiar sound of a pistol firing. A bullet zinged past his head. The Nazi was a good shot, but not good enough.

They kept running into the trees, the shadows of the forest swallowing them up.

❖ ❖ ❖

"I think they're leaving," whispered Mother.

Henri peered around the tree root behind which he and Mother huddled. She was right—the two German soldiers were walking back to the checkpoint, kicking at grass angrily as they went. From what he could hear, even Monsieur Barteau, their driver, had safely escaped while the soldiers were focused on them.

The Nazis were mostly angry at not having caught Mother—if Henri knew his German numbers right, there was a hefty bounty on Mother's head, more than five million francs—but they said they'd try again soon once someone showed up with more supplies and a search party.

One word Henri heard louder than others.

Hund. German for dog.

Part of him wondered if they had Brigette with them, or if one of the German battalions had her as a hunting dog. He had heard stories before, about the Nazis taking dogs and brainwashing them to be vicious hounds. Bri was probably a fantastic asset, a dog who knew France very well, and would know the places that German dogs weren't aware of.

Henri wondered what would happen if the Germans returned with Bri on a leash, blood-thirsty and brainwashed. If his faithful dog would be sent into the woods to hunt him and Mother. What Bri would do when the rebels she'd been trained to attack turned out to be the boy who loved her more than anyone else ever could.

His eyes stung as he remembered the day they'd taken her away. They had come by the house to question Father about Mother's where-abouts; they hadn't yet discovered that British journalist Linda Martin was the infamous White Fox, but Hitler's people had their suspicions. The officer from the SS that came to speak to Father wore a long black leather coat and had a silver skull on his hat that seemed to smile wickedly down at Henri. The officer had reminded Henri of pictures he'd seen in a magazine of the actor Bela Lugosi dressed as the vampire Dracula, with his cape spread about him like a bat's wings. That was what the Nazi officer looked like to Henri— like an angel of death, with cold eyes and black wings.

Father had turned them away firmly, knowing

they had no proof (that was Father, brave in the face of the Nazis—Henri couldn't believe it when he'd told Mother he would stay in Paris to help the Resistance groups in the city). Mother was good at hiding her involvement in the Resistance, and she certainly never brought her secret work home with her. But Brigette, Henri's half-collie, half-Doberman mix, had caught the officer's eye. He'd said that such a dog would better suit Hitler's needs than the Martins'. One of the soldiers had yanked her out of Henri's arms by the collar, and Henri had called him a rude German word that one of the boys in his class had taught him, which made Father chuckle and the officer sneer. Father had to wrap his arms around Henri's waist and hold him back as they dragged Bri away. Then he'd patted Henri's hair and shushed him while Henri wept for hours.

Bri, his sweet dog. He hoped they didn't have her. He hoped she'd escaped, hopped on the back of a truck, and was chasing chickens on some farm in the south.

"I think we're all right," said Mother. She and

Henri stood and stretched their limbs. Monsieur Tardivat and Monsieur Anselle crept out from their hiding places behind trees. Tardivat smiled at Henri and pretended to wipe sweat from his brow.

Anselle didn't share his compatriot's sense of humor. His eyes darted around the forest, and his hands clenched and unclenched at his side.

"This is a disaster," said Monsieur Anselle. "How are we meant to get these plans to Fécamp? We are done for!"

"Oh, quit your whining, Anselle," said Monsieur Tardivat. "This is a minor setback. We've been in tighter fixes than this."

"But not when the White Fox has been *made*!" said Monsieur Anselle, pointing at Mother. "That soldier recognized her. That means the Nazis are sending her picture around. She's meant to get us out of any situation. How are we supposed to get to Fécamp if every German soldier knows her at a glance?"

"I assure you, Monsieur Anselle, I am much more than a pretty face," said Mother, crossing her arms. Henri did the same, standing tall and straight at Mother's side.

"Sadly, Monsieur Anselle does have a point," said Monsieur Tardivat. "Now that you've been identified, your usefulness to us has changed—"

"It hasn't changed the fact that I can speak eight languages, forge federal documents, and knock a man out with my bare hands," snapped Mother. Henri smirked. He loved watching her stand up to the men in the Resistance, many of whom thought she was less skilled because she was a woman. They didn't know what they were talking about. Mother was a trained combatant, journalist, and spy, ready for anything. She'd seen more battle than most men had dreamed of.

"My apologies, Madame Martin," said Monsieur Tardivat. "But still, the issue remains. This puts everyone you know in danger. Your husband in Paris—"

"Antonin is safe with the Paris Resistance," said Mother. "He can handle himself, and he respects me enough to know I can do the same."

"Very well, then," said Tardivat. "But then what are *we* to do? We are meant to bring these plans to Fécamp and then meet the rest of the

Resistance fighters at Amiens tonight. Without the truck, the journey will take hours, perhaps even a day. The Resistance fighters in Amiens will get nervous and might abandon their post. Our contacts in Fécamp will not know where to meet the Allies coming their way. And now that the Germans know who you are, our chances of talking our way into a ride cross-country are poor."

Mother frowned at the men but said nothing. Henri knew that face—she didn't want to admit it, but they were right. Now that the Nazis knew that Linda Martin was the White Fox, Mother couldn't sneak her way through blockades the way she used to.

He was also right that they had to act fast. Anselle and Tardivat were important men, but if they showed up in Amiens without Mother, it would be a problem. The White Fox was more than just a spy, she was a symbol. Her presence meant they had a fighting chance, that they were under the guidance of one of the Resistance's best. But first, they needed to get to Fécamp and deliver plans for navigating the upcoming invasion by the Allies. Getting discovered at the checkpoint could throw their schedule off dangerously, especially if the rumors Henri had heard—that the Allies were planning a massive assault in the next twenty-four hours—were true.

Henri thought. There had to be a solution. They needed to go to both Fécamp and Amiens at the same time, but the Nazis were looking for Linda Martin and her Resistance fighters.

But, he thought, they weren't looking for him.

"I'll go to Fécamp," said Henri.

All eyes turned to him.

"What?" asked Monsieur Tardivat.

"I will bring the plans to Fécamp," said Henri. Part of him wanted to take back his offer the minute he spoke it, but he held fast. "The Germans will be so busy looking for the White Fox that they won't notice some French boy wandering through the countryside. This way, you can meet up with the Resistance cell in Amiens while I get the plans to Fécamp."

For a moment, Mother seemed pleased by

Henri's bravery—but then the scowl returned to her face.

"Absolutely not," she said.

"I second that," said Monsieur Anselle. "The boy cannot keep from talking in his sleep. It would be foolish to trust him with such a valuable mission."

"My son has seen more missions than you ever will," snapped Mother, but then quickly added, "though that does not mean he should go on this one. I brought him along to get him out of Paris, not to send him into the countryside alone. Besides, the soldiers who just recognized me will no doubt spread the word that a little boy came with us."

Henri looked to Monsieur Tardivat, who rubbed his chin in deep thought. Since Paris had been occupied and he began helping his Mother with missions, many Resistance fighters had scoffed at Mother bringing a child into the fold . . . except Tardivat. Tardivat had always been friendly to Henri. He taught Henri to fight, swim, and distract oncoming soldiers.

"It might work," mumbled Tardivat.

"It will not *work*, because it won't happen," said Mother.

"Linda, listen to me," said Tardivat. "There are lots of French children in the countryside—orphans whose parents have been captured by the Nazis. Henri could easily be mistaken for one. If anyone can get to Fécamp and give our contact his information, it's Henri."

"He's . . . easily distracted," said Mother, looking away from Henri. Henri felt stung that she would put him on the spot like this, in front of two members of the French Resistance. Was this about the time he'd left the stove on? Half of the curtains had been burned!

"Linda, if they had caught us back there, they would've caught him too," said Tardivat. That got her: Mother closed her eyes and breathed out slowly at the idea. "This way, he is separate from us. We go to Amiens and help our men prepare for the Allies landing in the morning. Our contact in Fécamp gets his information and arranges the meeting points along the coast."

Monsieur Tardivat went to Henri and knelt in front of him. Tardivat had a tough-man's face, thought Henri, with sleepy eyes, a firm chin, and a small mouth drawn in a tight little line. But somewhere behind that was what the Resistance was made of—a love of life, a hatred of bullies, a belief in freedom.

And, Henri saw, a belief in him.

"What do you think, my friend?" he asked. "Are you up for it?"

Henri felt scared of the idea now that it was becoming a reality—but he swallowed his fear. This was war, and there was no time to be scared at war. He wanted to help however he could.

"I'm in," said Henri.

He looked to Mother. Her tough expression was totally gone; now she stared at him with soft eyes glistening with tears. After a moment, she wiped them away with the backs of her hands and huffed a frustrated breath. She was the White Fox once more.

"All right then," she said. "Anselle, get out the maps. My son must know where he's going if he is going to help bring down Hitler once and for all."

CHAPTER 3

Ace was just dozing off when Jake came barging into their room. At first, Ace just raised his head, a little annoyed at having his nap interrupted. But then he picked up on Jake's grin, heard the fast beating of his heart, smelled the sweat on his brow.

It triggered something in Ace, and he leaped to his feet and gave Jake a quick questioning bark.

Could it be? Could it *finally* be? No, no way. Ace shouldn't get his hopes up. He'd thought it might happen before, and then it got canceled . . .

But when Jake spoke to him, Ace couldn't believe his ears.

"Ace," said Jake, "it's time. It's time to go"—Jake's grin grew a little wider—"on the mission!"

The mission!

Finally! It was happening! Oh boy! Ace ran around the bed in a circle, barking for joy!

How long had they waited? How long had Jake trained him? How long had they eaten this base's terrible food, waiting for some sign that it was finally go time? There were only so many nights Ace could sneak into the same bag of stale oats before he needed a little more!

Adventure! Activity!

His own parachute!

It was finally happening! Ace was beside himself. No more practice runs, no more flights to get him used to the noise, no more close calls—he was parachuting into battle!

Ace leaped into Jake's arms, and Jake laughed and fell back on the bed, wrestling Ace back and forth and lifting him in the air while making plane noises. Ace could tell that Jake was as ready to go as he was—or at least close to it. NO ONE was as ready for the mission as Ace! But Jake had suffered through it all with him. It had been a full six months since Ace had left his family in Cleveland.

There had been a lot of emotional ups and downs since he left the family. First, Ace was scared to be leaving everyone. Then, he was frantic to get to work. THEN, he was sad when he had a hard time getting used to the noise of the plane—and then he was overjoyed on his first parachute ride down! Finally, he'd been disappointed to learn that their previous missions had been canceled.

But now it was all happening!

As Jake jumped up and began raiding his closet, Ace danced around him and barked. Good old Jake, as smart and fun as any human Ace had ever encountered. He couldn't wait to get to work alongside his friend.

"We're scheduled to land just after oh-one hundred hours, Ace," said Jake. "Air support first, with amphibious craft following. That is, if the weather holds. It's supposed to storm like crazy!"

Ace just barked agreeably. He couldn't really

understand Jake's human speak, but he got *to land, air,* and *weather,* so he had the basic idea.

Jake grabbed Ace's tin and tossed Ace one of his favorite snacks, a Judy Junker's Tasty Treat! That had to be a good sign—Ace only ever got one of those if he was a good boy or if Jake was about to ask him to do something dangerous and stupid.

If it was time for the mission, that meant both!

Ace jumped and caught it in midair to show Jake just how ready he was. He savored the salty, fatty tang of the treat; it reminded him of week-old bacon from behind the trash can, only better. Jake laughed and gave him a pat on the head and a "good boy."

See? It was time!

Then the fun part! Jake got down on his knees and held up Ace's parachute harness.

Ace knew he shouldn't waste any time getting ready for the mission—but he couldn't help himself. He danced back, crouched, and stuck his wagging tail up in the air to make sure Jake saw it.

Jake tilted his head and did his best to hide his smile. "*Aaaace* . . . ," he said.

Ace barked back. *Come and get me!*

With a laugh, Jake launched himself at Ace—but Ace nimbly dodged out of the way! It's what he was trained for, after all. Jake let Ace know just how happy he was by absolutely trashing the room—throwing the bed over, knocking boots and papers out of place, all while Ace easily dodged his reaching arms. Every time Ace dodged, Jake laughed a little louder.

Finally, Ace decided enough was enough, and he let Jake catch him. Jake knelt down, put Ace on the floor in front of him, and held out his harness.

"Ace!" he said. "In!"

Ace knew what to do next—he turned until he was facing away from Jake, and then he hopped up on his back legs. Jake pulled the vest around his arms, then whistled and slapped the ground. Ace hopped up on his front legs and dropped his back legs into the harness. Then Jake strapped him in, and he was ready to fly!

Once Jake was dressed in his own harness, he whistled for Ace, and the two headed out into the hall and strutted toward the hangar. As they walked, they passed other rooms where the men were putting their uniforms and parachutes on. Many of them leaned out of their rooms and slapped Jake on the arm or whistled at Ace.

One soldier, a friend of Jake's named Tommy, came running out and put his fists up, like he wanted to fight. Ace hopped up on his back legs, spun his front paws, and gave a little growl. Tommy cackled, put his hand on Jake's shoulder and said a lot of fast, loud human words. Ace understood the important ones—*Mission. Ready. Fight. It's time!*

Ace couldn't be more ready. His mind reeled with questions: Where were they were flying to? What smells would be there? Would other dogs be there? His training told him there would be—mean dogs, enemy dogs that were trained to attack them.

Well, let 'em come! Ace didn't care. As long as he was by Jake's side, everything would be all right.

He could smell the rubber and gas of the big plane room down the hallway when a master stepped out and called, "Jake Tanaka?" Ace recognized this master by his smell—he was an older master named Holloway, who didn't much like Jake, and especially didn't like Ace.

Masters like Holloway, Ace knew, never came with good news. He hoped Jake would be okay.

Holloway approached Jake, and they spoke some human words—and then they both looked down at Ace. Holloway gave Ace the usual mean eyes, but Jake looked at him with sadness and worry. Holloway kept talking, but Jake just kept looking sad.

Ace gave a little whine and tilted his head. What was wrong? Someone in trouble? Another dog he had to work with? Whatever it was, they could handle it. He and Jake against the world, right?

Jake turned around. Whistled for Ace. Walked back to the room.

Oh no! Ace jumped in front of Jake and barked. It couldn't be! No mission? But—but it was finally time! What was wrong? Jake shouldn't listen to that Holloway master, he was all bad news and old smells!

They got back to the door to the room. Jake opened the door, pointed inside.

"Go, Ace," he said, sounding sad.

Ace looked into the room, then back at Jake. He didn't get it. Why him first?

Oh. *Oh.*

There was still a mission, but it was a Jake mission.

Not an Ace mission.

Jake knelt down and petted Ace's head. Ace could tell it was hurting Jake inside almost as much as it hurt him.

"I'm sorry, Ace," he said. "No mission today. This one isn't for dogs." He sighed. "You would've made a great soldier, Ace."

Ace's heart sank. He whined like some little puppy. It was embarrassing, but he couldn't help it. All this time, it had been about the two of them together, and now . . .

"TANAKA!" called Holloway. Jake looked to the voice, then back to Ace. He knelt, picked up Ace, and hugged him close. Ace licked his face . . . but it was no use. Jake put him down and mumbled, "Good boy, Ace."

Then he closed the door behind him.

Ace jumped at the door and barked. No! It wasn't right! How would Jake make it through the mission without Ace? Who would look for booby traps or do a perimeter check? Who would pee on the enemy's stuff, to let them know it belonged to Jake and Ace now? This was a disaster!

Ace whined. He knew that being a good boy meant *lie down and go back to sleep.*

But in times like this, sometimes it paid to be a bad dog.

Ace crawled under the bed and found the hole in the wall. It had been here when they'd gotten the room; he didn't think Jake even knew about it. Sure enough, it led to a narrow passageway inside the wall. Ace carefully shimmied, making sure not to catch his parachute on the edge, and then he was running through the dusty darkness, using his ears and nose to guide him.

Ace made several turns, walked through huge billows of dust, and even scared away a huge rat— before he closed in on the sound coming from a slotted window.

There! Through the slots, he could see the

plane room. And there, getting onto the plane, was Jake!

Ace threw his body into the metal window and felt it budge. He did it again, and it budged a little more. One more time—

BANG! The window flew off.

Across the room, the hatch of the plane was already closing. If Ace waited one more second, it would close and he'd be left behind. Head down, he ran with all his might.

CHAPTER 4

Henri checked the compass and map he'd been given. That patch of thick woods up ahead should be the forest Mother had drawn as a big dark circle. He could skirt around the side of it, pass one road beyond it, and eventually hit a crossroads. From there, he'd head northwest, and he should reach Fécamp by midnight.

The sky overhead was dark gray and rumbled with thunder. He rolled up the map and tucked it in his coat pocket, next to the leather satchel containing the secret plans. A cold breeze blew past, making him shiver. He could smell the rain coming, somewhere between the smell of wet stone and a dirty penny. He hoped the weather would hold and keep him from getting soaked.

Henri moved faster, trying to keep himself warm and buck up his spirits. What was a little rain? Here he was, running a solo mission for the French Resistance! Not even men like Monsieur Anselle were asked to run solo missions. Being entrusted with this responsibility meant that Mother and Monsieur Tardivat believed in him as a freedom fighter. To think that someday, when the Nazis were finally overthrown, he would be remembered as a hero.

IF, he thought, *not WHEN we overthrow the Nazis, but IF*. That was something Mother said to correct freedom fighters getting ahead of themselves. The world owed them nothing, and you never got anywhere on luck and chance alone. Expecting things to turn out your way was dangerous.

It certainly *had* been, the last time France had ignored a threat.

No one had expected Hitler would ever rise

to power in Germany. And even after he had become chancellor, plenty of people had laughed at the idea that he would attack a country like France. But then he'd attacked—first Poland, then Czechoslovakia, then France. Henri remembered the first time he'd seen Nazi soldiers in the streets, marching with their black boots sticking straight out.

And then, destruction. Violence. Nazis at every door, interrogating people the Martins knew. Dragging away friends, family, neighbors, coworkers . . .

Even family dogs.

Henri tried not to think of Brigette, but he couldn't help himself. He'd had her for five years, since he was six. Bri had been his best friend, running with him through the streets of Paris, playing catch with him and the other boys, charging out to greet Mother every time she came back from a "business trip" (what he was meant to call her Resistance meetings).

Brigette had been wonderful—smart, kind, and loyal. Henri had trained her to jump, sit, roll over, and shake. He had fallen asleep many nights with his head lying on her shaggy black coat. He had never been happier than he was with his trusted dog. And he hadn't been happy since she'd been stolen.

Henri felt the backs of his eyes sting. He shook his head, trying to shake away the sad thoughts. He couldn't get distracted. Mother had told him, over and over—*Do not get distracted. Don't talk to strangers. Don't investigate noises. Go straight there as fast as you can.*

Even before Bri had been taken away, it had been a problem for Henri. He liked to daydream, to relive old memories, and to see what was going on when he heard a loud noise. His natural state was running, jumping, and bending down and peering into things. But since Bri had been taken away, it had gotten worse. All he could think about was how much he missed her, to the point where his teachers, friends, and Mother and Father had to shake him out of his bad moods several times a day. Any time he heard a noise, a rustling of papers or the tap of a branch at the window, he thought, *Maybe it's her. Maybe she's found a way back to me.*

He couldn't get distracted now. Too much was at stake.

Henri could see the road from the edge of the woods, and he picked up the pace. He had to try and gain as much ground as he could before it got dark. The last thing he wanted was to get caught in the rain in pitch blackness.

As he got close to the road, Henri pulled out his map and studied it again . . . but then he saw something out of the corner of his eye that made him freeze.

CHAPTER 5

By the side of the road crouched a little girl. Her dress was stained with dirt and sweat, her shoes were worn, and her bob of dark hair was tangled and clumped. She was clawing through the grass, looking for something . . . but what?

Henri watched as she grabbed a few strands of tall grass and yanked them up out of the ground. At the end of them was a small white bulb, covered in dirt—a wild onion.

The girl brushed it off with her hand and brought it to her mouth.

"Hey!" said Henri. The girl leaped and spun to face him, putting the onion behind her back. As he walked toward her, Henri could see her green eyes staring wide and bright from under her ratty bangs. She was afraid of him.

"What are you doing?" he said. "You can't just eat that out of the ground! You have to wash it off first. And you should cook it too."

The girl was silent for a moment, and then she said softly, "Where can I cook it?"

"Why . . . your home, of course," said Henri. "Your mother can . . ."

The girl's eyes gleamed with tears. The words Monsieur Tardivat had spoken to Mother came back to him. This must be one of the children he'd mentioned, who had fled into the country-side when the Nazis had come for their families. No wonder she was looking for wild onions—she might not have eaten in days.

Henri was torn. On the one hand, he felt sorry for this little girl and wanted to help her. On the other, he couldn't get sidetracked. He had to get to Fécamp as soon as possible. He had to go now. All of France was counting on him . . .

But, he wondered, what good was he as a savior of France if he couldn't help one little girl?

"Here," he said. He tucked his map under his arm, fished around in his coat pocket, and found the half a baguette and piece of cured beef that Mother had given him for the journey. He ripped a piece off of each and held them out to the little girl. At first the girl didn't move . . . and then she darted forward and snatched them from Henri's hand!

Before Henri could say a word, the girl shoved the food in her mouth and made little whimpering noises as she chewed them.

"Slow down," he said. "If you don't chew enough, you'll get sick."

"Thank you," said the little girl, spitting crumbs.

"You're welcome," said Henri. "What's your name?"

"Elle," said the girl.

"You should find a hiding spot," said Henri. "There are Nazis in this area, and there's rumor of a big attack by the Allies coming soon. You need to get somewhere safe."

"How do you know the Allies are coming here?" she asked.

"I'm a resistance fighter—" Henri slapped his hand over his mouth. What was *wrong* with him? He'd just blown his cover to a stranger! She could be a Nazi spy, posing as a lost little girl! This was exactly what Monsieur Anselle had talked about!

If Elle was a Nazi spy, she didn't act it—instead, she cocked her head and frowned at Henri. "You don't *look* like a Resistance fighter. You're just a kid. They don't just let boys as small as you fight for the Resistance."

Henri's cheeks burned. He wasn't *small*! Who did this girl think she was? He opened his mouth to tell her she didn't know what she was talking about—

When the sound of a horn in the distance made him stiffen.

Henri looked over his shoulder to see a Nazi convoy heading their way.

What could he do? Part of him wanted to bolt into the countryside. But that went against Monsieur Tardivat's training. *Never run if you don't need to*, he had taught Henri. *Keep your cool. Running just lets them know you're up to something.*

He turned back to Elle, to tell her to be quiet and let him do the talking. Before he could, she threw a handful of dirt on to his shirt and smeared some on his cheeks.

"What are you doing?" he hissed, slapping her hands away.

"They need to think you are an orphan, like me," whispered Elle. "You look too clean right now. Just rub the dirt around. You'll be fine."

That's actually a good idea, thought Henri, though he felt a little offended by having to be told what to do by some orphan. There was no time to argue—the sounds of the trucks' motors filled the air. Henri smeared dirt on his face and hoped he looked hungry enough to pass as Elle's brother.

There were eight trucks in all. On the doors were painted huge white circles with black swastikas in them, and in the back of each truck sat about thirty German soldiers with rifles. The soldiers all glared at him as they rolled by. Henri noticed that some of the soldiers had dogs too—Doberman Pinschers, with sharp upright ears and

pointed faces. It was hard to believe that a dog as soft and sweet as Brigette had been the child of a dog so angular and scary-looking as a Doberman.

The first seven trucks passed them . . .

And then the eighth stopped.

The whine of the brakes made Henri cringe.

His map, tucked under his arm, tumbled from his grip . . . and dropped slowly into the mud.

CHAPTER 6

"You! Boy!"

Panic shot through Henri. The map sat at his feet, half unfolded. The Nazis were yelling for him. The directions were written in French, not German, but one of them could no doubt speak French.

He had to hide it . . . and there was only one way he could think of.

Henri felt his heart ache as he moved his foot over the map and stomped it into the mud. Then he forced himself to look up at the Germans.

The truck sat rumbling in front of them. Soldiers filled the back, as well as two Dobermans with hard black eyes and Iron Crosses dangling from their studded collars. They all eyed Henri and Elle with utter contempt.

The soldier who spoke to him leaned out of the truck's passenger window. He carefully observed Henri and Elle from behind round spectacles.

"What are you two doing on the road?" barked the soldier in heavily accented French. "Do you have your papers on you? Where are your parents?"

Henri searched for the right words, but it felt as though his mouth were full of gum. He was messing this up!

Thankfully, Elle stepped forward and spoke. "My brother and I are on our way back to Dieppe, sir," she said. "Our parents sent us out to look for wild onions for their soup." She raised the dirty onion she'd almost eaten.

"Well, you'd better start heading back there if you want to make it home before dinner," yelled the soldier. "And tell your parents not to let their children run wild throughout the countryside." A cruel grin grew across his face. "Don't you know there's a war on?"

"Yes, sir," said Elle. "Are you going to Dieppe? Perhaps you can give us a ride home—"

"I can't be taxiing every lost child across France," said the Nazi. "Just head home now. And tell your parents to keep you inside, or else you might catch a bullet. As long as you stay east of Le Havre, you should be fine."

The soldier gave Henri one last long look, and Henri was terrified that the soldier had heard stories about the White Fox traveling with a small boy . . . but then he sat back in his car and gave his driver a swat on the arm.

"*Heil Hitler,*" he snapped, and then the truck roared off down the road. It followed the other trucks in the convoy around a bend . . . and out of sight.

At once, Henri fell to his knees and dug the sodden map out of the mud. He tried to be careful with it—but as he lifted it, the soaked paper ripped in half in his hands. He held the torn pieces for a moment longer before letting them fall back into the dirt.

Henri felt as if he were falling down a bottomless pit. This couldn't be happening. He tried to remember the instructions on the map—the crossroads was . . . through the forest? Was there another road before this one? No, that wasn't right. Was Fécamp east of Le Havre? No, he didn't think so . . .

Tears stung the back of Henri's eyes, and his breath hitched in his chest. He was lost. He had failed Mother. If he ever got to Fécamp, it would be too late. The Resistance wouldn't know where to meet the Allies, and France would never be free of the Nazis . . .

"Are you all right?" asked Elle. "What's that paper?"

"Leave me alone," said Henri, doing his best to swallow back his sobs. "My map is ruined. My mission is over. I'm totally lost. I'll never make it to Fécamp in time without it. I have no idea where to go."

"I know how to get to Fécamp."

What? Henri's eyes darted up to Elle as a flicker of hope lit up inside him. For her part, the little girl stared down at him as though he were some sort of bug she'd never seen before.

"You . . . you do?" He sniffed and rose to his feet. "Can you lead me there?"

"Sure," she said, waving him along. "You gave me some of your food—it's the least I can do. Quickly, though, it's a long walk."

Elle started walking, and Henri jogged up next to her. This was amazing! The mission was saved! He still had a chance of getting to Fécamp and giving the plans to Mother's Resistance contact. To think that if he hadn't been nice to this girl, he might be stuck out here alone, surrounded by Nazis and unfamiliar countryside.

Henri's spirits began to pick up. Life had a funny way of working out. He wasn't a failure, he'd just had to think on his feet. And hey, he'd also learned some vital intel—as long as they didn't go east of Le Havre, they had a good chance of being unbothered for the rest of the night. If he stayed the course, and Elle knew where she was going, this should be an easy journey.

As they walked out into a grassy field, Henri felt the first raindrop plop coldly against the back of his neck. Elle must have felt one too, because she looked up at the sky and frowned.

Well, maybe it wouldn't be so easy after all.

One by one, fat raindrops began plopping down onto Henri and Elle. Soon, the sound of their drumming filled the countryside. Then all at once, it was pouring, the rain beating down on them, the ground turning muddy beneath their feet. Thunder boomed in the sky.

"It's not so bad," Henri told himself, trying to stay hopeful. "It's just a little rain. Nothing to worry about—"

BOOM! With blinding flash, a bolt of lightning struck a tree some hundred yards away, sending a shower of sparks into the air. Then Henri and Elle ran, hoping to find shelter, as the terrible storm seemed to attack them from all sides.

CHAPTER 7

Ace knew what was about to happen long before they opened the door to the plane. Over the new rush of sounds and smells—the booming outside the plane that made the walls rattle, the sharp peppery blasts of powder and carbine—he picked up on the soldiers' nerves. Their hearts were pounding. Their toes were tapping. Even Jake, at whose feet Ace rested, was sweating profusely.

Ace didn't understand. Only hours ago, when he'd come trotting out of the ammo compartment,

Jake had been overjoyed. All the men had been, laughing and petting him and cheering him on for finding a way on board. He'd even fake-boxed with Tommy a little. But now they were terrified. That made no sense.

Besides, this was the mission, right? This was what they'd been waiting for, for months! Why would they be frightened? Sure, it was dangerous, but that's why they'd been training . . .

One of the other masters shouted at the men. At once, they all stood and created a line in front of the plane door. Jake was last, and he looked back at Ace with wide, frightened eyes.

"Ready, Ace?" he said.

Ace barked at him. Of course he was ready! Why wouldn't he be? What was the big deal about—

The master in front threw open the door to the plane, and the noise blasted in. The air howled, and in it screamed and roared dozens of bombs and giant artillery shells. It was so loud that Ace couldn't help but jump a little.

This was much scarier than training.

Maybe he wasn't so ready after all . . .

One by one, the men leaped out of the plane and vanished into the night sky. It was exactly like the exercises they'd performed back at the base . . . only it was so much darker beyond the door than it had been during training. The noises coming from the sky outside were closer than they'd ever been.

Without meaning to, Ace whined and began inching away toward the back of the plane.

One of the other masters tapped Jake's shoulder and pointed at Ace. Jake looked back and tried to smile at Ace. But Ace could tell it wasn't a real smile—it was fake, the same smile Jake gave Ace when Ace had to go to the vet or be locked up for the night.

Ace whined. He wanted to be brave. He *was* brave. But . . . he was scared!

The master yelled something. Jake walked back to Ace and picked him up.

"Don't worry, Ace," said Jake. "It'll all be okay. I promise."

Ace whined. He wasn't as ready as he thought he'd be. If he could just have a few more minutes—

"Three . . ." yelled Jake.

Wait . . . no! Ace began to wriggle in Jake's hands.

"Two . . ."

Jake stepped up to the door.

Oh no. Ace felt his heart beating so fast he was worried it might burst. He whined without meaning to. His feet spun in the air. They were—Jake was—

"One . . ."

Ace barked—*Wait, wait, wait!*

And then Jake jumped, and in midair he let Ace go.

Wind filled Ace's ears and stung his eyes. He howled as the night rushed around him, a blur of black. There was a swooping noise, and then—

TWANG! The straps on his harness pulled tight.

Ace was airborne! He sailed through the sky at the end of his parachute. Now that he wasn't falling, it wasn't so bad! It was just like training!

A shell whizzed past Ace and exploded behind him, making him yelp. Okay, maybe not *exactly* like training.

He looked around him, trying to make sense

of what he was seeing. On his sides, the men were hanging in the sky from their blown-out parachutes. In the clouds between them, light flickered—both long strings of lightning and quick bursts of gunpowder. And down on the ground below, Ace could just barely see the men landing, discarding their parachutes, and running for cover.

That's where they needed him—on the ground, with Jake, doing his job! Ace sniffed the air, trying to pick up Jake's scent again. All the other sounds and smells were too much for him, though, and he couldn't get ahold of Jake's smell.

Oh no! Had he lost him? Was he already ruining the mission?

If only he could get down on the ground quicker!

Ace wriggled and bounced, hoping to make his descent go a little faster—

SNAP!

One of his parachute straps broke. Ace swung hard to the side. All at once, a gust of wind hit him and yanked him away from the men, off into the chilly darkness of the clouds.

Ace spun and whipped through the air. He barked, but no one responded to him. He couldn't smell Jake, or the men, or the plane—or anyone! The whole world spun around him as he plummeted into the night.

He was going down!

CHAPTER 8

OUTSIDE RICARVILLE, FRANCE
MONDAY, JUNE 5, 1944
11:11 P.M.

The sky gave them everything it had.

Rain pounded the earth. It swept across the countryside in waves. Huge gusts of wind blew up, blasting droplets directly in Henri's face. He hunched his shoulders and tried to remain calm, but he felt as though he might burst into tears at any minute.

Elle had led them to the crossroads, and the flame of Henri's hope had roared when he saw signs for Fécamp. But as the rain got worse, the road had become a swamp of giant puddles and miniature rivers that rushed by at surprising speed. Meanwhile, the grassy countryside along the roadside grew loose and muddy, threatening to suck the boots off his feet any time he left the packed dirt of the road.

They found a ramshackle barn along the side of the road and stopped to dry off a little and catch their breath. They shared the remainder of the meat and baguette, though the bread was soggy. Henri found an old piece of tarp in one corner and wrapped it around his secret plans. He stuffed them deep in his coat pocket and hoped that was enough to keep them safe from water damage.

As Henri stared out at the lightning streaking across the sky, his thoughts turned to Mother. A veil of worry dropped over him that felt as cold and wet as his soaked clothes. He hoped Mother had made it to Amiens safely, and that she wasn't too worried about him. He knew he should just focus on the task at hand—Mother was an excellent spy, and she could handle herself—but he couldn't help but wonder what might have happened to her. Hearing that Nazi soldier recognize her had shaken his resolve a little. Suppose they caught her on the road. Suppose she stopped at a farmhouse and asked for directions, and the farmer had ratted her out to the Nazis. Suppose . . .

He had to stop. He couldn't think about it. It was too terrible, and it didn't help him at all. Getting to Fécamp was all that mattered.

Henri heard a ragged breath and chattering teeth. In one corner of the barn, Elle huddled on a bale of hay, her knees clutched to her chest. The sight of her all wet and cold saddened him. He thought of what Mother would want him to do in this situation.

"Here," he said, taking off his coat. He shook as much water off of it as possible, and then held it out to Elle.

Elle glared at the coat as though it might have a snake in it. "I'm fine," she said. "I've been on my own for a while. I've seen worse weather than this."

"You'll catch cold," said Henri. When she wouldn't take it, he walked over to her and draped the coat over her shoulders. Elle never stopped him, and though she didn't say thank you, Henri saw a soft look come over her eyes. It made him feel a little warmer than he had second before. "Think you're able to keep going?"

She nodded, and they headed back out into the night.

The darkness was deep and black, with the moon a faint smudge behind the clouds. The rain had become a fine mist. But that was almost worse—there was no avoiding the mist, no matter what tree or roof they ducked under. Cold had set in as well, and their breath came out in thick blasts of steam. Henri kept his hands shoved into his pockets and his body bent forward. Without his coat, he was freezing, but seeing Elle bundled warmly in it made him feel a little warmer.

Henri stared at the horizon. He wondered when they would finally see the lights of Fécamp in the distance. The town had to be close—bad weather or no, they'd walked far enough.

A brief burst of light made the horizon blink white. A loud thud echoed in the air.

"Not another storm," he grumbled, hunching his shoulders even higher.

But then he noticed Elle had stopped walking.

She stared into the sky, wide-eyed, and pointed out into the night.

"No storm," she said. "Look."

Henri followed Elle's finger and saw only endless black night. But then he heard the thudding again, and he saw another flash—only this one didn't come out of the clouds, it came from the ground!

Artillery. Somewhere off in the distance, big guns were firing. Shells were exploding. By the volume of the noise, Henri imagined they were still far away from them, maybe even five or six kilometers. Yet the way that they echoed and painted the countryside with their flickering light still made Henri worried. If he could see the explosions from this far away, who knows how big those guns were up close?

There was a blast of light in the air. For a split second, he saw round shapes among the clouds, like the caps of mushrooms.

"What are those?" asked Elle. "Balloons? Why would there be—"

As the realization dawned on Henri, a grin spread across his face.

"Not balloons," he gasped. "Parachutes!"

The Allies were parachuting in! Henri had heard Mother and Monsieur Tardivat talking about Americans invading Normandy for a while now. Even yesterday, they'd spoken about how there were meant to be assaults by land *and* air, with American, British, and Canadian forces arriving in big boats on the beaches of Normandy. But they'd doubted it would happen because of the weather. The Allied plans had already been rescheduled multiple times. No matter how bad the storm was in France, it was worse out at sea.

But here they were, parachuting down, braving both the terrible weather and the big German guns to try and get to them!

Another flash, and Henri saw even more parachutes against the fluffy clouds.

"Come on," he said, pointing to the hill along the side of the road. "From up there, we can get a better view!"

Henri ran off the road, splashing through puddles as he went, and moved to climb the hill—

STOP!

Henri froze. This was *exactly* what Mother

had talked about. He was getting distracted. The longer he spent staring at the battle in the distance, the longer Mother's contacts were waiting for him.

"What?" said Elle, coming up behind him.

"Never mind," said Henri, trudging back toward the road. "We can't get sidetracked. Let's go."

Henri got back on the road to Fécamp and turned to Elle . . . only Elle wasn't there. In a glimmer of light from the distant artillery, he saw that she had continued climbing and now stood at the top of the hill, staring off into the countryside. Henri cursed at himself for even giving her the idea of watching the battle.

"Elle, come on," he called out. "We have to keep moving."

"There's something in this tree," she replied. "Come quick!" And then she ran down the far side of the hill.

Henri groaned and went marching off the road and up the hill. He hoped Elle hadn't gotten *too* sidetracked. What could she have seen in that tree—a bird, maybe, or an old hunting blind? Or worse, what if it was an undetonated bomb? Mother had told him about those, how they'd sit dormant where they landed until a light jostle from a passing car made them go off. The thought made Henri jog a little faster. What a story that'd be—almost at Fécamp, and he got blown up because some orphan wanted to flick a lethal weapon.

As Henri crested the hill, the clouds finally parted, and the moon bathed the countryside in ghostly blue light. Up ahead, Henri could see Elle reaching for something in the branches of a dead tree—some sort of white clothing hanging in midair and shaking. It was almost as though a ghost had gotten caught on a branch.

"What is that?" he cried out to Elle. "Be careful!"

"We need to get him down!" she called back.

Him?

Henri came up beside Elle and looked up into the tree. There, hanging in a web of ropes and tattered white cloth, was a tiny dog, its body white with black spots. It had a small face and big eyes that reminded Henri more of a bat than any dog

he'd ever seen. It spun its little legs, making it swing from the ropes it was tangled in . . . no, not ropes, parachute cords! Henri realized that the dog was dangling from a parachute that was caught in the branches!

"Huh," he said, taking in the dog's parachute vest. He couldn't help but smile to himself. A dog parachuting into France under German fire! Who had heard of such a thing?

The dog barked again and spun its legs faster. The message was clear: *GET ME DOWN!*

Henri reached for the dog—but stopped midway.

"What are you doing?" asked Elle.

"We don't know whose dog this is," said Henri. "This isn't our mission. We have to get to Fécamp before—"

"Are you serious?" said Elle. "He needs our help! We can't just leave him there." She shook her head and started walking toward the tree. "*Not our mission.* Ridiculous. Just be ready to catch him when I'm done, okay?"

"What do you mean—" Before Henri could

finish the sentence, Elle took a running start and leaped to one of the lower branches of the tree. Her hands wrapped around it, and she pulled herself onto it. Henri had to admit, he was impressed by her climbing.

Elle shimmied out onto the branch from which the dog dangled. The little dog yipped and whined as Elle got closer. He even turned his head back and tried to nip at her, but Elle cooed, and whispered, "Easy, boy."

Slowly, she snaked her hands between the ropes that held the dog up. He heard the clicking of buckles, and—

SNAP! The dog's straps broke, and he fell to earth. Henri dove forward with his arms out and just barely caught the little guy. Then he went falling to the ground in a splash of icy mud.

As Henri stood and wiped the mud from his pants, Elle jumped down from her branch and knelt down next to the dog, who was wagging his tail and yipping at them.

"Hush, little friend," she said. "Hush . . ." Elle reached down to the dog's collar and checked the tag on it. "Ace?"

As if in response, the dog stopped barking and sat.

Henri tried to be stoic and wanted to insist they get back on the road . . . but he couldn't help himself. He reached out and scratched the dog behind the ear and on the hindquarters, feeling the animal's heart beating fast in his warm little body. The feeling of a dog, even a small, bat-faced one, reminded him of his time with Brigette. He smiled and laughed at the little creature, who bounced excitedly and yipped at them as though he hoped they understood dog.

"Where do you think he came from?" asked Elle.

Henri peered at the dog's green parachute harness. On the side, he saw black stenciled letters spelling UNITED STATES AIR FORCE.

"I think he's an Allied soldier dog of some sort," said Henri. It sounded silly to him, but all evidence pointed to that being the case. Using dogs during the war wasn't uncommon—even Mother's French companions had told stories of Chief, the British dog who'd survived the Blitz, and Skipper, the hero dog of Pearl Harbor. But dropping a dog out of an airplane? That sounded like a little much, even during a war!

Another shell exploded in the distance. Immediately, Ace turned to it and began barking.

"Aw, he probably misses his platoon," said Elle. "Don't worry, boy, we'll help you find them." Ace barked louder, and angrier, and she picked him up and held him. "It's okay, boy, we'll get you—"

"Wait," said Henri. "Shush."

Henri lifted his ear to the air. Had he been hearing things? Maybe it had just been some shell fire, or the whistle of a bomb . . .

Then he heard it again. This time there was no mistaking it. And the surprised expression on Elle's face told him he wasn't just imagining things.

Another dog was barking back. By the sound of it, a bigger, meaner dog.

And it was getting closer.

CHAPTER 9

"**R**un," said Henri.

He and Elle jumped to their feet and ran as fast as they could, and Ace followed behind them. Any worry about heading in the right direction to get to Fécamp exited Henri's mind in a flash—all that mattered now was getting somewhere they could hide.

A voice in Henri's head mentioned that he had just found a dog dangling in a tree, so perhaps this was another American parachute dog. Maybe the

Allies were dropping dogs all over France to aid in the war effort . . .

But no, that was wishful thinking. After years of owning Brigette, he could tell a happy bark from an angry one. Whatever other dogs were coming after them, they were not friendly. And they were not small either.

Freezing cold mud splashed up around them as they ran, soaking Henri's trousers and dripping into his boots. Up ahead, he could see a patch of forest, sparse but full of tall trees. If they could make it there, they could hide, or even climb up a tree. Then everything would be okay, at least for a little while . . .

Next to him, Elle's foot sank into a deep puddle and caught. She went falling to the ground with a cry and a splash.

Henri came to a halt and reached down to try and help her. Ace was leaping back and forth, barking at them as though to say, *Come on! We have to go! There's no time!*

A patch of deep mud had swallowed Elle's one leg up to the calf. Henri helped Elle pull her foot from the puddle, but her shoe stayed mired deep in the muck. He grabbed it and yanked, and with a deep sucking noise, the shoe popped free.

"Thank you," she said, turning it upside down and pouring dirty water out of it.

"It's fine," he said through quick, heavy breaths. "But let's go! We need to get moving again before—"

Ace stopped yipping and growled. He dropped to a crouch and faced the road.

Slowly, dread rising inside him, Henri looked up into the blackness.

To Henri, the Doberman looked less like a dog and more like a weapon of war built by the Germans. Her pointed face reminded him of a machine gun bullet, and her ears looked like two pointed turrets on the side of a black fortress. Her broad chest jutted out proudly and led to a sleek body full of muscles that would probably allow her to spring through the air with deadly grace.

In a blaze of lightning, Henri even saw the name printed on the Iron Cross hanging from its collar: KRIEGER. German for *warrior*.

The Doberman took a careful step forward and growled back at Ace—but her growl was far lower and scarier than Ace's. She sounded as though Ace were a whining mosquito and Krieger were a fighter plane. Henri was stunned by how brave Ace was being in the face of a dog so big and threatening.

Henri felt Elle tense against him and heard a sob hitch up in her throat.

"Don't move," he whispered. "If we just back away slowly, she might not attack us . . ."

His hopes deflated as he watched a pair of headlights come over the top of a hill in the distance.

An all-terrain truck roared across the muddy ground and over to where the Doberman was standing, so that the powerful dog became a silhouette in the glare of its light beams. As it came to a stop in front of them, Henri saw the white circle with the black swastika inside of it printed on the doors.

Fear gripped him, cold and terrible.

There was no escaping them now.

"Hands where we can see them!" screamed one of the two Nazis who leaped out of the truck's cab. Both men had their Luger pistols drawn, and they wore long black raincoats that made them look like smokestacks with feet and helmets.

Slowly, Henri and Elle raised their hands. Henri didn't know what else to do. He felt utterly defeated. What would Mother say if she could see him now? She'd be embarrassed by him. Ashamed that he was so easily distracted by a little parachute dog hanging from a tree, and so easily caught by the enemy.

One of the Nazis instructed them to walk toward the truck. The other one approached Ace, who snarled and darted forward as if to bite his hand. But the soldier was quicker, and he grabbed Ace by the back of his neck. The little dog's legs wheeled helplessly as the Nazi raised him high in the air.

"Another hound for the ranks!" laughed the soldier in German. "And look at this, Peter—he wears an American uniform! He's some kind of spy-dog from the States!"

"Doesn't matter where he's from, Reinhardt," snapped the Nazi pointing his gun at Henri and Elle. "All dogs become obedient to the Third Reich once they're broken."

"What do we do with the children?" asked Reinhardt.

"Let's bring them with us," said Peter. "For all we know, they're spies themselves. If we have to deal with any of those American swine, they might make good hostages." The Nazi grabbed Henri by the shoulder and shoved him toward the truck. "You, in the back. On the double."

Henri and Elle sat perfectly still as the truck rumbled across the countryside. Ace barked from the cage he'd been crammed into, while Krieger the Doberman sat nearby, watching over them.

The sounds of the battle got louder and louder as they drove, and the flickering lights in the clouds got brighter. Wherever they were going, Henri knew it was in the opposite direction of Fécamp.

Henri couldn't believe it. Captured by the

enemy. Being taken, well, who knew where? He was a terrible freedom fighter. Sooner or later, one of the soldiers would no doubt find the plans he was trusted with tucked away in his coat, now wrapped around Elle. They would figure out where the Resistance cells were going to meet the Allies, and all of the invasion plans would be lost. And Mother . . .

Henri bit his lip and clenched his eyes hard. Even if Mother was ashamed of him, he just prayed she was okay. If there were Nazi dogs roaming the countryside, she might have been caught before getting to Amiens. But hopefully only he was so stupid and unlucky to be caught on this mission.

Elle put a hand on his shoulder. "Are you all right?" she whispered.

"No, I'm not," he muttered through his tears. "You wouldn't understand. Everything's gone wrong."

Elle was silent for a moment and then said, "They took my mama and papa away in a truck like this. I might understand."

Henri sniffed and looked into the little girl's

sad eyes. He hadn't even thought about Elle's family. That was unfair of him to say, even if he was upset . . .

The truck lurched to a halt. Henri looked over the cab and saw that they were parked in front of a concrete bunker, square and bleak. Instead of windows, the little building had long slits in the walls, out of which stuck the barrels of heavy mounted machine guns. Off in the distance, glimmering faintly in the moonlight, Henri could make out the ocean.

The Nazis climbed out of the cab and came back to the bed of the truck.

"Reinhardt, get the brats out first," said Peter. "Then the little American dog. If he bites you, shoot him."

"Leave him alone, German pig dogs!" shouted Henri in his best German.

Peter sneered at him. "Don't worry, little friend," he said. "As long as he behaves himself, your little dog will only be thrown in a cage for a while."

The sneer became a grin. Peter held up two

pairs of handcuffs and a couple of black sacks. Henri's breath caught as he recognized the black cloth bags, like small pillowcases—hoods. The kind the Germans put over your head before marching you through town . . . and taking you away forever.

"You two, on the other hand," said the Nazi slimily, "might not be so lucky."

CHAPTER 10

Ho boy. This, this was gonna be a problem.

Ace growled under his breath as the enemy soldier carried him into a little stone house that smelled of moldy boots and live ammunition. Beside him, the enemy dog trotted, giving off a scent that was equal parts confidence and anger. Ace could tell this "Krieger" dog (what kind of a name was that?) didn't get a lot of love or Judy's Junker Treats the way he did. The enemy dogs were probably raised the way the mean dogs in his Cleveland neighborhood were—a lot of slaps to the snout and kicks to the stomach. He'd feel sorry for them if they weren't so mean.

If only he hadn't gotten blown off course . . .

This was what he deserved, he told himself. Punishment for his moment of shame, when he'd finally faced the mission and had let Jake down. Instead of jumping on his own, he'd backed away in fear, like some . . . some *cat*.

He was so embarrassed.

Scared of jumping. Getting blown off course. Having to be rescued by some human pups. Then getting captured by the enemy.

He was so worried about Jake. The mission called for Ace to be doing all sorts of tasks for Jake right after they'd landed. First, Ace was going to check for any oncoming soldiers. *Then* Ace was going to suss out any enemy dogs and lead them on a wild chase before narrowly escaping them and returning. *THEN* he was going to lead the pack and notify Jake of any tripwires, mines, or other booby traps that the enemy had laid for them on the beach—all before they headed to the meeting point!

What if Jake had gotten caught on a tripwire,

setting off some booby trap? What if he'd stepped on a mine? Was he remembering to smell for carbine so he knew other soldiers were coming?

And what about peeing? How was the enemy going to know that Jake had taken the beach if someone didn't pee on it? He knew Jake would forget. He was a great guy, but really terrible about marking his territory. That was Ace's job.

But where was Ace?

Ace was in some horrible little stone base, under the watchful eye of the enemy.

Some soldier he was.

The man carried Ace into the dark little room. Around them, other enemy soldiers stood in their black uniforms, like shadows with eyes and voices. They manned big loud guns like the ones Jake had trained Ace to dodge. Ace could smell anger and discontent on the enemy shadows. He wasn't surprised. Through the short, wide windows in the stone wall, he could smell all sorts of wonderful things—wet grass, cows, and, off in the distance, the delicious saltiness of the ocean. Instead of getting to enjoy the country, these masters were forced to be in here, surrounded only by weapons.

The enemy shadows yelled human words he didn't understand and pointed to the pups who'd saved Ace. The shadow holding him laughed and dangled him over the enemy dog at his side. The enemy dog growled and snapped, and Ace had to pull up his butt to keep from getting bit.

The pups, Elle and Henri, shouted from under the black hoods over their heads. One of the enemy shadows shouted back, and he swatted Henri upside his head as though he were a bad dog. Elle cried out, and she got swatted as well.

Ace growled.

Those human pups had saved him from that tree. They'd been nice to him. They had given him scratches behind his ears—the ultimate human-to-canine display of loyalty and affection. And they'd done nothing to deserve "bad dog" swats.

Now it was personal.

The enemy shadow carried him down a flight of stairs and into a basement even more damp and cold than the room upstairs. Another enemy dog was down there, chained to a wall and wearing a muzzle. The enemy shadow holding Ace tossed him into a little rusty cage in one corner and locked it. Then he shoved the pups into a taller cage—it was obviously meant for only one human, but he forced them to press tightly together. He used metal contraptions to lock their hands behind their backs, rendering them powerless. Then he locked the cage, put the keys on his belt, and left.

Krieger, the enemy dog who'd caught them, stayed behind, and watched them attentively with her pointy face and hard, stony eyes.

Ace surveyed the scene—and found it pretty miserable. Elle was crying softly. Henri was trying to say soothing things to her in the tone of *Good girl* and *It's okay*, but he wasn't very convincing. One horrible enemy dog was watching him, while the one chained to the wall . . .

That dog was watching the boy.

Something was up with that other enemy dog. Ace couldn't put a paw on it quite yet.

But he couldn't worry about that now. He needed to get out of here. Something Jake had taught him was that when the mission changed, you had to come up with a new plan.

So maybe the plan had originally been to help Jake and protect him—but now it was to help these human pups. They'd been kind to Ace. They'd saved his life, even though it meant getting caught and swatted by these horrible enemy shadows. And they might be able to help him further, if he could get them free.

Time for Ace to do his part.

They needed a way out—and that was Ace's specialty. He'd snuck out of every room, kennel, and cage he'd ever been locked in. Heck, he'd snuck his way onto a plane and behind enemy lines. It was just about finding the weak spot.

Ace laid down on the dirt floor of his cage and thought . . .

Oh, of course!

A dirt floor. These masters had been too lazy to cover the floor of this little bunker's basement, and his cage was planted in the floor with long spikes, so it had no bottom. He'd just dig his way out, and—

The enemy dog, Krieger. That would be an issue. She was big, strong, and mean. The minute he started digging, she would hear him with those big pointed ears and push her big head into his cage, and . . .

Just like that, the new plan came together in his head. Ace couldn't help but wag his tail a little at the thought. If it all worked out, this would be fun.

Ace barked at the front of his cage and made the first few scrapes with his paws at the bottom edge, creating a little gap between the bottom of the cage and the floor.

This got Krieger's attention—she stood and growled low in her throat.

Now Ace had to work fast! He began digging quickly, scraping up big pawfuls of dirt and making a noticeable little tunnel under the edge of his cage. He needed to make the hole big enough, but not too big.

Krieger began barking loudly. Ace could smell her anger at him.

That was good. He wanted her angry. The angrier she was, the less she would think. The less she thought, the easier it would be to trick her into falling for his trap.

The hole was *just* big enough, Ace thought.

He ducked down and put his head into it, peeking out at Krieger from under the bottom of the cage. He panted, wagged his tail, and yipped at her. *Come and get me, stupid. I'm about to escape.*

Krieger snarled and lunged at Ace's face. At the last minute, Ace pulled his face back and leaped to the side—just as Krieger shoved her pointed muzzle into the hole. Now her head was all the way into Ace's cage, snapping and snarling.

When it was obvious she couldn't get Ace, Krieger grunted . . . and froze.

She tried to pull back out of the cage—but her head and ears weren't as pointy as her snout, and they caught on the bottom bar. She pulled twice, making the cage rattle, but couldn't go anywhere. She was stuck!

Ace's tail wagged like crazy. The trap had worked perfectly!

Quick as a flash, Ace dug another hole on the other side of his cage. Then he got down on his belly and crawled under it. Bam, he was out! Krieger barked angrily, but with her head stuck between the cage and the ground, she wasn't much of a threat to Ace.

Ace turned to face the other enemy dog . . . but once again, she didn't seem very interested in him. All she did was stare at the boy, the way Ace might stare at Jake. What was going on? She could just be an especially bad enemy dog, but Ace thought there might be something else . . .

Never mind. Not important. He could solve that mystery later—for now, he needed to get the human pups out of this room.

Ace thought back on his training. First step, trap or disable the enemy. Good, done. Second, escape. Bingo, done. Next, help your crew. The human pups were locked in their cage with a big, heavy padlock. He needed to get those keys that were dangling from the enemy shadow's belt. That would be easy enough—and then all he had to do was send them on a chase.

He crept up the stairs stealthily, doing his best to keep his toenails from clicking on the metal beneath them.

At the top of the stairs, three enemy soldiers stood around talking. The two who'd brought them here were still dressed in their shadow-wear, but the third and fourth were dressed like typical soldiers, in green uniforms with tall black boots.

There, from the one enemy shadow's belt, hung the ring of keys.

Ace looked around the room. This was something he'd always impressed Jake with—using the room to help him escape. There was always a way out that only Ace saw.

After a few seconds, the plan came to him. It would be tough, and timing was essential—but if he played it right, this plan would be spectacular. Maybe the greatest escape he'd ever pulled off.

First, the easy part.

Ace darted across the room to the enemy shadow with the ring of keys on his belt. For a split second, the enemy shadow's face twisted up, like he couldn't quite believe what he was seeing—and then Ace grabbed the keys and ripped them from his belt. The enemy shadows had barely enough time to shout before Ace leaped up to one of the thin windows in the stone wall and squeezed out into the open air.

Now the tricky part!

The minute Ace hit the grass, he laid down

as low as he could—belly on the ground, limbs out flat, head so far down that the grass crunched beneath his chin. Then he waited.

Sure enough, the enemy soldiers came bumbling out, shouting at the top of their lungs and pointing off into the distance. Ace couldn't understand their words, but he knew what they were saying. He'd seen Jake's officers act the same way in the past during training exercises. *He went that way!* they were yelling. *See, look at the grass? Quick, we need to catch up with him!*

Ace watched as one by one, the enemy shadows went running out into the night, looking for him. He wagged his tail. Making them chase you was easy, but making them chase you when you never went anywhere? That was a skill.

And look, they didn't even close the door behind them! Ace had been worried about hopping back up into one of the windows, but those silly masters had made it easier for him.

As Ace trotted back into the building, he felt mighty proud of himself . . . until he got back to the basement and saw the human pups with the bags over their faces. The Krieger dog was grunting as she began to inch her head out from the crevice in which it was stuck.

There was no time to be proud. He had to get the pups out of there now. Their lives depended on it.

CHAPTER 11

Henri wasn't sure which he felt more: fear or confusion.

On the one hand, he was very scared—for himself, for Elle, for Mother and her companions, for all of war-torn France.

On the other hand, *what was going on out there?*

With the hood over his head, Henri was living in a world of insane sounds. First, there was barking in the room around them—and then that stopped, and there was only the sound of a dog whining and grunting. Suddenly, from upstairs, he heard all sorts of shouting and the stumbling of boots. Then the whole commotion moved outside and went quiet.

"Henri, what's happening?" whispered Elle from under her own hood.

"I don't know," Henri whispered back. He wished he had an answer for her, but he was clueless. What sort of commotion had overtaken the bunker? Had the Allies landed nearby? It certainly sounded like a battle.

Suddenly, Henri felt something cold and metal being pressed against his thigh. He turned so he could touch it with his cuffed hands, and his fingers felt out the shape—and found a ring of keys!

Could it be?

Excitement surged inside him, but he did his best to keep it at bay. Part of the training he'd done with Mother and Monsieur Tardivat was to keep his head about him, both when things seemed too terrible or too good to be true.

But they had also taught him how to get out of handcuffs. And if there was a key small enough on this ring, then . . .

Carefully, so as not to drop them, Henri felt his way through the key ring and found a small key. He twisted his wrists, wincing as the metal of the cuffs bit into his skin.

Almost there . . .

The key entered the cuff, and with a twist his one wrist was free!

Quickly, Henri unlocked the other cuff and yanked his hood off.

He'd expected to see a lot of things . . . but he hadn't expected this.

They were in some moldy dirt-floor storage basement beneath the bunker, lit by a single dismal bulb. The walls were lined with concrete and stacked high with crates of ammunition and crates of rations. A short ways away, Krieger, the scary Doberman who'd chased them down, was crouched with her head stuck underneath a small kennel attached to the floor, while another dog was muzzled and chained to a wall across from them. And up against the bars of his own cell stood . . .

"Ace!" cried Henri with a laugh. He reached through the bars and petted Ace's chin. "How'd you . . . what did you . . . I can't believe this!"

"What's going on?" asked Elle.

"Ace saved us," said Henri. He quickly unlocked Elle's cuffs and then got to work on the large padlock holding their cell shut. The first key didn't work . . . the second didn't work . . . but the third slid right into it and clicked the lock open. And just like that, they were out, with Ace dancing around their feet, yipping excitedly.

"Come on, we need to get out of here while the soldiers are still busy," said Henri. He and Elle walked between the two Nazi dogs toward the spiral stairs.

The muzzled dog chained to the wall moved to Henri with a whine and nuzzled his fingers. Henri instinctively yanked his hand away, worried the enemy dog was trying to bite him.

Then he saw her eyes.

Those eyes.

His mind was playing tricks on him. It . . . it couldn't be.

"Henri?" asked Elle. "Henri, please, we need to get moving."

But Henri couldn't look away from the dog's

huge, soulful eyes. Eyes he saw in his memories, in his dreams. Eyes that he'd missed for months.

"Bri?" he whispered. He dropped to one knee and held her face in his hands. "Brigette, is that you?"

She whined at him and nuzzled his face. The leather of her muzzle scraped against his cheek.

"Henri, come," hissed Elle. "That dog could be dangerous! It could—"

But Henri wasn't listening. His hands shook as he grabbed the muzzle's buckle and unlocked it, letting it fall to the ground in front of him—and instantly, Brigette's tongue was all over him, giving him countless kisses on his face and neck! It *was* her!

"Oh, Brigette!" cried Henri, feeling tears come to his eyes. He buried his face in her neck, breathing her in. All this time later, she still smelled the same. "I knew I'd find you! I knew you'd come back to me!"

"Henri!" said Elle.

Henri forced himself to think clearly. Elle was right, they needed to leave at once. But he wouldn't do it without Brigette. He unbuckled

her collar, freeing her from the wall. She walked forward with a bit of a hobble, her one front paw bandaged. He noticed that the Nazis had given her an Iron Cross and a stupid war name—BLITZ, German for *lightning*. Under hers, though, was a paper tag, handwritten in German:

Disobedient—injury sustained during training. Terminate when convenient.

His skin crawled as he read the tag again, to make sure he'd seen it right.

Henri felt anger burn behind his face. Monsters. The Nazis were nothing more than barbaric monsters trying to take over the world in the name of evil. They couldn't even leave his dog alive.

"Let's go," said Henri. He slapped his thigh, and Brigette and Ace followed close behind him as they tiptoed up the stairs.

The top floor of the bunker was exactly as Henri had imagined—full of ammunition crates, with a huge swastika flag hanging from one wall. A mounted heavy-artillery machine gun with a long metal barrel was aimed out of a wide, thin window along one wall, facing toward the ocean. This must be one of the Nazis' gun emplacements, he realized—a miniature base along the coastline where German soldiers could pick off any incoming attacks from the Allies.

Henri glanced at the crates along the walls—MG42 bullets, antiaircraft rounds, *Stielhandgranate* grenades. Whatever the Allies had in store, the Germans would be ready for it.

The more Henri stared at the weapons, the more he swelled with anger.

These bullets would be used to kill Allied soldiers trying to save France. They would be used to kill any French people who got in the Nazis' way. If it hadn't been for Ace, they would've been used to kill Brigette . . . and maybe Henri and Elle.

He wouldn't let them do any more damage.

Henri went to the crate marked *Stielhandgranate* and opened it. Stacked on top of each other were German hand grenades. Each one had a broad, cylindrical body and a long handle like that of a rolling pin. Dangling out of a hole in the bottom of a handle was a string.

Monsieur Tardivat had taught him about

these. All he needed to do was pull the string . . .

Henri picked one up. He was surprised at how heavy it was in his hand. He'd have to throw it hard back through the door . . .

From down the stairs, there was a loud bark. At his side, Ace and Brigette crouched and growled.

"Come on!" Henri yelled, lugging the grenade in his one hand. As they ran out the door, he could hear the sound of toenails on the metal steps below.

They were at the door when Krieger came charging up the stairs. Having her head stuck beneath the cage must've made her angry, thought Henri, because the Doberman looked scarier now than she did when she had first caught them. Her lips were peeled back in a toothy snarl that trailed foam behind it as she ran.

Henri cried out as Krieger launched herself into the air and leaped right at him.

CHAPTER 12

A white blur flashed in front of Henri and knocked Krieger out of the air.

The Doberman tumbled to the ground, rolled on her back, and regained her footing.

In front of her, Ace crouched with a snarl, squaring off against the dog twice his size.

"Ace, stop!" cried Henri. But it was no use— Ace was ready to fight, and Krieger wanted payback. Brigette barked at his side and darted forward, but the minute she put pressure on her bandaged paw, she stumbled and yipped. Krieger

shoulder-checked her aside and went back to Ace.

Ace snapped at Krieger, and the two dogs launched at each other, standing up on their hind legs. They snarled and bit at each other. Krieger seized Ace by the back of the neck and threw him against a wall. Ace slammed into it with a yelp. He immediately jumped back to his feet and barked, but Henri could see the red pinpricks from where Krieger had bitten him.

"Henri, do something!" cried Elle, but Henri was helpless. Part of it was because he knew they should flee the scene, run off into the night, put as much distance between them and the bunker as possible . . . but part of it was because Krieger was so terrifying. Ace and Brigette were brave, but the Nazis' Doberman had been trained as a tool of destruction. Trying to get between her and her prey might result in Henri losing a hand.

"HEY! STOP!"

Henri wheeled. In the moonlight, he could make out shapes charging across the countryside. He recognized their voices—it was the Nazis who had captured them.

He thought quickly. If they didn't leave, they

might get caught again. If he didn't use the grenade, the Germans would have all the weapons in the world to attack him with. And if he didn't do something soon, Ace might get killed by Krieger.

Henri turned to Elle. "Elle, when I say go, run. Run as fast and as far as you can away from this bunker. Don't look back—just go!"

"No!" she said. "I'm not leaving you behind!"

"It's the only way for us to escape," said Henri. "This way, they won't know who to chase. If you can, head to Amiens. Find my mother, Linda Martin. She'll help you."

"Henri, *please*," she said, tears spilling down her cheeks.

There was the sound of a gunshot, and the dirt at Henri's feet spat up a tiny cloud.

"Next one's in your stomach!" shouted one of the Nazis. This close, Henri could see their eyes in the dark. They were narrow and mean, full of hate and planning something terrible for Henri and his friends.

He raised the grenade into view and watched their anger give way to fear.

"Run!" shouted Henri.

It all happened so fast: Elle ran into the dark. Henri pulled the string on the grenade and threw it as hard as he could into the bunker, where it rolled down the spiral stairs. The Nazis all dropped to the ground, hands over their heads.

"ACE!" screamed Henri.

Krieger lunged for Ace, but he was faster than her. The little dog bounded out of his enemy's path and ran for the door. Krieger turned, snarling, and pursued him.

Henri turned and sprinted, hoping he and Ace could make it out of range before he heard the—

KABOOOM!

The shockwave lifted Henri off of his feet and sent him sailing through the air. For a moment, the night around him lit up as clear as day.

Then Henri crashed to the ground and rolled in the dirt, scraping his elbows and knees as he went. When he stopped moving, he put his arms over his head as small pieces of concrete and shell casing rained down over him.

Finally, as the downpour of wreckage ceased, Henri looked up at his handiwork.

Where the bunker had stood, there was only

a giant fireball billowing up into the night. All of the gunpowder and grenades stored inside were catching, and every few seconds a new blast of heat and noise would light up the sky and reinforce the raging flames.

Henri scanned the world around him. Elle was nowhere to be seen, and if the Nazis hadn't gotten blown back by the blast, they were staying put. That left . . .

"Ace?" he called out. "Brigette?"

He heard a bark.

There. Henri's eyes found Brigette standing a few feet away. She barked at Henri and nuzzled a small shape on the ground.

It was Ace.

And he wasn't moving.

CHAPTER 13

Ace sniffed the air. What were those familiar smells?

The blur in his vision came into focus.

It was the house in Cleveland!

Ace finally put the smells together—the grass from the yard, the rust from the tire swing's chain, Reggie's baseball glove sitting on the front porch, the lake off in the distance. He was back home!

Everything was just as he remembered it— the old flaking wood of the house, the fence on either side blocking out the Dericksons' stupid cat

Bobbo. The way the afternoon light warmed him and the breeze blew the grass on the lawn meant only one thing: it was almost time for Reggie to come home from school. Then they would play fetch, and afterward, Ace would get his evening meal. Then he and Reggie would curl up in front of the radio together, and he'd get some long, slow scratches behind the ear.

Ace took a step toward the house . . .

Ace!

He froze.

No. This . . . this wasn't real. It was all in his head. He didn't know *how* he knew . . . but he knew.

He wasn't back in Cleveland, he was in enemy territory, on the mission. The boy he was protecting wasn't Reggie, it was Henri. Henri and Elle. They'd saved him from the tree. He'd helped them escape their cage.

And then, when that evil Krieger had tried to attack them, Ace had faced her. He hadn't tricked her or escaped her, he'd fought her, like a big dog. Like a hero.

Because he was sick of running away. Because

some dogs didn't need to be tricked or taught a lesson, they needed to be fought. Because when the time came, he knew he would give everything to save those two human pups who had been so good to him.

It was what Jake would've wanted him to do. Not just Jake, but the family back in Cleveland too. They would've all been proud of him.

Ace!

Henri's voice.

Ace looked back at the Cleveland house. It was so perfect, so beautiful. If he went there, he could just roll in the lawn and play forever . . .

But not today. If he could hear the boy's voice, there was still a mission. And he would let no dog say that Ace abandoned his post.

He turned away from the house, kicked some dirt at it with his hind legs . . . and headed back to the world.

Ace woke with a snort. He shook his head and sat up.

Yikes. Everything hurt. That dog had really walloped him.

He lay cradled in Henri's arms. The boy gasped to see him wake up, and he said his name over and over again—"Oh, Ace! Ace! Ace!" He clutched Ace tight, and Ace couldn't help but yelp as pain shot through him. He'd taken a pretty bad beating against Krieger, he knew, but there was also an ache in his one front paw that made him think things had gotten even a little crazier.

Ace felt a lick on his snout, and he looked up to see the other enemy dog, the one who had been acting so strange in the little stone room. She sniffed curiously at him and whimpered, and he sniffed back. All he got were happy smells— happy smells for the boy, and happy smells for him still being alive. She was a good dog, he decided, and gave her a tiny lick on the nose.

"Good girl, Bri," said Henri.

Aha—she was the human pup's dog! The enemy must have captured her, the way they'd captured Ace. Wow, the enemy did *not* like this human pup!

The human pup put Ace down, and though he had to bend his one paw, Ace could still hop without it hurting too badly. He took a moment and used his nose and ears to fill out the scene around them.

The stone building sat off in the distance, spewing fire and smoke into the air. The enemy's car had also caught on fire and was burning into the night. The whole scene was a long walk away—at least a mile. Henri must have carried him the entire time.

Things *had* gotten crazy! What else had Ace missed while he was out? He turned around with a grunt, faced away from the fire and toward—

The water!

Ace barked for joy! The ocean! That meant the beach—which is where the mission was! He was supposed to be on the beach this whole time! If he could get there now, he might still be able to find Jake and the rest of the men!

Ace looked back to Henri and Bri and barked for them to head toward the beach. Bri understood him, but she looked to the human pup for agreement. Henri seemed unsure.

"No, Ace," he said. "That's where the fighting is."

Ace barked—*exactly!*

"No, Ace," he said again, staring away from the ocean into the field. "We need to get moving. We need to . . ."

Ace could see how tired the human pup was. He needed to buck the kid's spirits up. Carefully, moving his wounded paw as little as he could, he hopped up on his back legs and spun on his legs, growling.

Henri laughed. Ace saw a little joy come back into his face.

"Good boy, Ace," he said.

Ace got back down on his three good legs and swung his head at the ocean with a quick bark. And this time, Henri nodded. He started out toward the sea, and the dogs followed.

By the time they got to the coastline, Ace wondered if going to the beach was a good idea.

To their one side, the night continued booming and flickering with gunfire, and every few seconds there was the sound of a voice shouting or screaming. Up ahead, the ocean stretched out for miles, lit by a rippling line of light . . . but Ace could also tell that it wasn't safe there either. The ocean was dark and deep, and in it, far off, there were ships moving around.

Ships full of Allies, yes—ships full of men speaking the same human language as Jake and Tommy—but ships of battle nonetheless.

Ace looked to Bri, and the bigger dog shot him back a similar frown of worry. If only they could tell Henri. If only they could let him know that out on the ocean, ships full of soldiers, weapons, and destruction were on their way to this very shore? That off in the dark, more stone houses full of guns and enemy shadows were lurking in the countryside, looking to attack people like him—

Tripwire!

The smell of copper wire set off an alarm in Ace's head. There, only a few feet in front of them, a length of metal was strung across the path. On one side, a wooden post held it up. On the other, buried in the ground, was a bomb.

Ace hopped out in front of Henri and barked loudly. Henri shushed him—obviously, in the dark, he couldn't see the danger.

Ace signaled him the way he'd been taught to: he crouched down and began sniffing at the wire, moving back and forth in a line. Then he hopped over it and performed the same action from the other side.

Henri only looked confused—until Bri joined in! She approached the wire, sniffed it back and forth, and backed up to Henri and whined. Henri crouched, reached carefully forward, and gently touched the wire. His hand snapped back, and he stood and took a wide step over the wire.

"Good boy, Ace!" he whispered in the dark. "Good girl, Bri!"

Ace joined Henri at his side, giving a little snort of approval to Bri. Maybe they couldn't tell Henri about the noise and violence that was on its way, but they could protect him from the danger in his path.

That was all they could do. But it was enough. It had to be.

Because the danger wasn't over. Ace's training didn't tell him that. There was no smell or sound that alerted him to it. He just knew, in that way that dogs knew things when humans didn't. That way that told him it was near suppertime, or that an invisible bit of a master who had died remained in some part of a house.

There was danger ahead. And they had to be careful if they wanted to survive it.

CHAPTER 14

Henri had been to Fécamp once before, when he was two. He only knew this because Mother had told him about it when they were getting ready to escape Paris. *We're heading to Fécamp*, she'd said. *Remember, we went there for holiday once? It's a sweet little seaside town. We went fishing and sailing. It was so much fun. You had a wonderful time.*

Now, in the dead of night under stormy skies, Fécamp was anything but sweet. The yellow light from the gas lamps along the streets threw creepy shadows that made every alley look like a grave. The houses against the hills were all dark and looming; some were half destroyed, with piles of rubble and broken furniture where there should be walls. The harbor sloshed and sucked at the beach, and it smelled more like gas and gunpowder than it did like salt water and fish. Lines of sandbags topped with barbed wire sat along the outer streets. Here and there a red banner bearing a black swastika fluttered in the damp breeze.

Henri pointed and whispered, "We're here, dogs! Fécamp!"

But the dogs didn't seem excited. Ace glanced around and growled, while Bri shot Henri the worried expression she sometimes wore when Henri had to go to school and leave her alone all day.

"Come on, Ace," he said, leaning down and scratching him behind the ear. Then he made sure to give Bri a scratch, so as not to make her feel left out. *Mon Dieu*, first he had no dogs, then he had too many to handle. What was the expression? When it rained, it poured!

Henri tiptoed down the silent streets, keeping

his eyes peeled for patrols just as Mother and Monsieur Tardivat had instructed. He could see his meeting point in the distance—the inn, one of the few places in the town with a light still on in its window. As he got closer and closer, his heart swelled with pride, but he was also a little sad. He had reached his destination, but his journey had been hard. He had only wanted to help the Resistance, not blow up Nazi bunkers. Not get his new dog friend hurt fighting with a terrifying Doberman.

Henri thought of Elle, the girl who had helped him get across what felt like half of France and had comforted him when he felt scared. He worried about Mother, who may have heard that he had not reached Fécamp in time. He hoped they were all safe, that Mother and Elle had not been intercepted by the Nazis.

Henri sighed. All this war. All this hate and pain. He just wanted to take his dogs and go home. But these were the times, he knew, when you had to keep going. When you had to sacrifice all you had for something bigger than your comfort or your safety. Because it was right.

Henri got to the inn's front door and rapped it three times—*bang, bang, bang.* And seconds later, a man with a big round belly and a mustache opened it and stared down at him with a smile.

"Why, a little boy and his dogs!" he laughed in a kind voice. "What are you doing here?"

"I am looking for Bertram, owner of this inn," said Henri.

"I am Bertram," said the man, snapping his suspenders proudly. "And yes, this is my inn. But, my boy, this is no place for children at this time of the night! The tavern is closing soon, and our kitchen has been silent for hours. If your father is in here, I promise I will send him home with a cup of coffee in him—"

Henri spoke the secret code Mother and Monsieur Tardivat had taught him, word for word: "I have been told that white foxes only hunt at night."

Bertram's smile dropped. His air of fun and kindness vanished. "What is this? Who are you? Where is Linda? Where is Tardivat?"

"I am Henri Martin, Linda's son," whispered Henri. "She has sent me in her place."

Bertram glared at him suspiciously. Finally, he

said, "You have the plans?"

Henri opened his mouth, reached for his coat pocket—and felt the blood drain out of his face.

The plans. The plans were in his coat pocket.

His coat was on Elle.

He couldn't believe it. All this way, and he had forgotten the *one thing* he was supposed to bring to the Resistance. Somehow, despite defeating a group of Nazi soldiers, saving an orphan, and finding his long-lost dog, Henri had *still* managed to get distracted and ruin the mission. Right now, maybe the most important document in all of France was running around the countryside in a damp coat on a frightened girl.

He stared up into Bertram's expectant face.

What could he possibly say to this man?

"The plans . . . are gone," he mumbled, his lips numb. "I was in danger, and they were in my coat . . . and my coat was lost."

For a moment, Bertram looked livid with rage—but then he huffed and shook his head.

"Where is your mother?" he asked.

"In Amiens," said Henri in a shaking voice, feeling suddenly very cold and very alone. "We split up so I could get the plans here while she met with our contacts in Amiens. But . . . but . . ."

"That was smart," rumbled Bertram. "Meeting the Resistance group in Amiens was more important. All right, look, from what I've heard earlier tonight, the Allied invasion has already begun. Let me get my jacket. I will drive you to Amiens, and we will meet with your mother. She'll know what to do—"

All at once, Ace began barking at the top of his lungs and hopping around on his healthy legs. Henri shushed him, but the small dog kept yipping in a panic.

"Shut that dog up!" hissed Bertram. "We can't be discovered now!"

Henri heard the click of a pistol hammer.

"I think, *mein Freund*," said a familiar voice, "it's a little late for that."

CHAPTER 15

The pit in Henri's stomach grew deeper and deeper as he and Bertram put their hands up and stepped out in front of the inn.

The four Nazis from the bunker—Peter, Reinhardt, and the two infantrymen—stood around them with Luger pistols raised. Peter had the barrel of his gun inches away from Henri's face. All the men looked like they'd been left in the oven too long. The edges of their coats and uniforms were singed and blackened, and they had dark ash smeared on their faces.

"I guess you were a little too close when I set off that grenade," said Henri, glaring at Peter.

Peter's mouth curled into a smile that had no warmth in it. "A sense of humor until the very end." He nodded to his men. "Now."

One of the infantrymen came up to Bertram and jammed a pistol in his belly.

Peter grabbed Henri by the collar, spun him, and put him in a headlock. Henri fought against him—until he felt the cold metal of the pistol against his temple.

Bri and Ace barked and tried to defend him, but the other infantryman stormed forward and gave Bri a sharp kick in the ribs, making her cry out and tumble to the cobblestones. Reinhardt, the other officer, picked up Ace by the back of his neck; when Ace twisted and tried to bite him, he gave the dog a hard shake, making Ace yip at having his wounds from earlier jostled.

"Leave them alone!" cried Henri, feeling hot tears pour down his face. "They're just dogs!"

"They're an enemy of the *Führer* is what they are!" snarled Peter in his ear. "If it were up to me, I'd toss them into a pit and let both of them starve to death!"

"Please," Bertram blubbered, "please, sir, I'm just a lowly inn owner, I don't know what you mean—"

"Quiet, you traitor!" shouted Peter. "We heard your little talk. Planning to meet up with your friends in the Resistance, eh? After we take care of you and your little traveling companions, perhaps my men and I will swing by Amiens and have a talk with the freedom fighters there."

"No!" screamed Henri. He twisted and fought against the Nazi's grip, but it was no use. Peter's hold was strong, and the metal of his pistol bit into the back of Henri's skull painfully.

"But before that," laughed the Nazi into Henri's ear, "we'll show you what a real dog looks like. Reinhardt?"

Reinhardt whistled.

Along the cobblestones, Henri heard the click of toenails. The jangle of an Iron Cross collar. A low, hateful growl.

By the looks of her, Krieger had only barely escaped the explosion. Patches of the dog's fur were singed and ashen. Her left ear looked red and raw. But her shining eyes still held all the same focus and fury that they'd had earlier in the night. As she walked toward her masters, she only gave a fleeting glance and a *ruff* at Bri before focusing on her real prey: Ace.

"Dinnertime," said Reinhardt, dangling Ace in the air.

Krieger came to Reinhardt's feet and stared up at Ace. She licked her lips, and great gobs of saliva ran from her chops and fell to the stones at her feet. Ace looked down at her with a little whimper, but then panted with his tongue out as if to say, *Here it is, ya Nazi mutt. Let me know how it tastes.*

Henri tried to look away, but Peter put a gloved hand on his cheek and turned his head back to the scene.

"You watch," he snapped. "Watch what happens to the enemies of the Third Reich."

"Krieger, sit!" cried Reinhardt in a jolly tone.

The Doberman sat. The Nazis all chuckled cruelly.

"Krieger, speak!" ordered Reinhardt.

The Doberman's growl turned into a single, roaring bark.

"Now, Krieger," said Reinhardt, "eat."

He began to lower Ace toward the Doberman's drooling mouth . . .

"HEY!"

Henri felt Peter tense behind him. Everyone froze and raised their heads at the sound of the new voice. Even Krieger hopped to her feet and looked around, as though interrupted during a private moment.

Around them, Henri heard the click of a gun being cocked.

And then he heard another. And another. And a dozen more.

A circle of soldiers closed in around them. They were dressed in the green fatigues and black strap-up boots of American paratroopers. All of them had M-16 machine guns and 9mm pistols aimed at the Nazi soldiers. At their head was an Asian American man with a furious expression on his face, who marched forward and squared off with Reinhardt so quickly that the Nazi officer took a bumbling step back.

From Reinhardt's raised hand, Ace barked happily and wagged his stubby little tail like a madman.

The American looked up at Ace, then back at Reinhardt. "I think you have something that belongs to me, buddy."

The Nazi handed Ace to the American soldier, who chuckled as the little dog excitedly licked his face and nuzzled his chin. The soldier glanced down at Krieger, who slunk slowly away from the confident American.

"Mean-looking animal you got there," said the American.

"Shoot her if you like," said Reinhardt in accented English, standing up straight and trying to appear tough. "But she will die as a loyal member of the Nazi Party."

The American scoffed. "You kidding? I'd never hurt a dog. That's cruel."

CRACK! His fist slammed into Reinhardt's jaw. The Nazi spun, took one unbalanced step— and then collapsed in a heap.

"A Nazi, on the other hand," grumbled the soldier, "that's a pleasure."

Everything happened around Henri in a flash—the Americans closed in on the Nazis. Krieger fled into the darkness of the town with a growl. Two paratroopers pulled Peter off of Henri and dragged him and his infantrymen toward the tavern. The Nazi gave a final pathetic *"Heil Hitler!"* before one of the American paratroopers gave him a hard flick on the nose.

The American paratrooper approached Henri with a big smile.

"Jake Tanaka," he said in English, extending a hand. "You Henry?"

As he shook the soldier's hand, Henri couldn't help but smile at the American's pronunciation. "It's Henri. French name, with an *i*."

Jake laughed and rolled his eyes. *"Henri,* then. Sorry, my French is lousy. Point is . . ." He reached into the breast of his uniform and produced a bundle of papers loosely wrapped in a tarp. "Are these yours?"

"Y-yes!" cried Henri, his heart soaring. "Only—how did you get those?"

"I gave them to him!"

Henri looked past Jake to see a small figure crouched next to Brigette.

A small figure . . . wearing *his* coat!

"Elle!" he cried, and without meaning to he ran to her and threw his arms around her neck. Elle giggled as he squeezed her tightly and then held her out at arm's length. It was the first time Henri had seen her smile.

"Careful," said Elle, gesturing to Brigette. "She's hurt."

Oh no! Henri knelt next to his dog and petted her gently. Bri licked his hand, but he could see by how little she moved and how she was breathing that the Nazi's boot had really hurt her. He stroked her face and cooed to her, and her tail thumped against the cobblestones.

"I think she'll be okay," said Elle. "She just needs to rest up."

Henri looked from Bri to Elle to Jake to Ace. His mind spun with a million questions. He went with the most pressing one:

"What . . . *happened*?" he asked.

"When I was running from the bunker, I got

picked up by Jake and his team," she said. "They had trouble with my French, but when they heard the name *Ace*, they realized that I had found Jake's dog. I told them your plans needed to get to Fécamp, and so . . . *voilà*!"

Henri couldn't believe it! Somehow, it had all worked out—he was reunited with Brigette, Elle had survived and made it to Fécamp, and the Allies had his Resistance plans. Someone upstairs must like him!

And yet . . . even through the joy of his victory, Henri's heart still weighed heavy. He stood and turned back to Jake, who was cradling Ace like a baby and scratching his belly.

"Have you heard any word from Amiens?" asked Henri. "From the Resistance cell there?"

"Not yet," said Jake. "But some of us are heading there next. Hold on, let me get these plans to my radio guy so he can reach out to our Resistance allies. Then we can give you a ride."

A few minutes later, Jake and some of his men helped Henri load Brigette into the back of Bertram's car, and they rumbled out along the country roads. Ace sat in the backseat with Henri and Elle. Every time they hit a hard bump and Brigette whined or yelped, the little dog would nuzzle her paw softly, as though to say, *Hang in there, soldier. We'll get you fixed up. Just a little ways farther.*

As morning light broke over the horizon, Henri heard sounds over the coughing of the engine. Shellfire cracking, bombs thudding, the whistle of heavy artillery shells flying through the air. Though the overcast sky only drizzled light rain, there was a never-ending sound of thunder. Henri stared out the back of the car and saw the dim morning light flicker with battle.

"I guess Operation Neptune has started." Henri turned to see Jake in the passenger seat, staring at him with a wise expression.

"It's happening, isn't it?" said Henri. "The Allied invasion. We're really going to take France back from them."

"France, Poland . . . we're taking it all back," said Jake. "We're burning their empire to the ground, kid. And we couldn't have done it without you."

Ace raised his head and grumbled.

"Or *you*, you whiner!" said Jake, and Henri let himself have a much-deserved laugh.

A half-mile outside of Amiens, the car began to slow down. Henri stared out the window and saw another team of American soldiers approaching them, along with what looked like several French freedom fighters.

Leading the team was a woman, her face smudged with dirt, a torn Nazi flag clutched in her fist.

Henri's pulse sped up. He breathed fast. A sob hit the back of his throat. And before he knew it, he was reaching for the door handle.

"Hey, kid, be careful!" yelled Jake as Henri leaped out of the still-moving car. He hit the ground running and sped across the grassy countryside as fast as he could. As he ran, he watched the woman's expression go from determined to shocked—and then she started running too.

They collided in the middle so hard that they nearly fell over. Both of them instantly burst into tears. Henri squeezed her for all he was worth.

She yanked him to her shoulder and kissed him hard on the top of his head.

"I did it, Mother," said Henri. "I did it."

"Oh, Henri," wept Linda. "My little hero. I knew you would."

EPILOGUE

PARIS, FRANCE
FRIDAY, AUGUST 25, 1944
1:00 P.M.

The sound of Brigette's nails clicking on the stone floor of the Palais Bourbon made Henri just the slightest bit self-conscious about her being here with them. They were so loud!

But he quickly cast away such thoughts. He wanted Bri out of his sight for as little as possible. And anyway, the general had insisted she come with them. Her legend was almost as great as that of the White Fox—the Parisian dog who'd escaped capture from the Germans and survived two fractured ribs from a Nazi soldier's boot.

Rumor had it that she was so disobedient, the Germans couldn't even use her as a guard dog. She'd earned her place in the Palais today.

"Down this way," said their guide, a skinny boy in a military uniform that didn't quite fit him.

"Thank you," said Mother. She reached out and squeezed Henri's shoulder. Henri smiled back, even though he was a little sick of being mothered lately. He would never say such a rude thing to her—he knew she was just feeling about him the way he felt about Brigette.

The scrawny soldier opened the door and ushered them into a large room covered with maps, blueprints, strategy boards, photos of well-known enemies and allies, and other bits of military data.

At the center of it all, a man hunched over a desk. When they entered, he looked up and smiled at them. He had a beaked nose, a sharp chin, and a thin mustache. But it was his eyes—bright and quick, but also a little tired—that really struck Henri. He thought that when you heard of a man having a *presence*, this was what they were talking about. The newspapers did him no justice.

"Linda Martin, at last," said the man in heavily

accented English.

"General de Gaulle," said Mother with a nod.

General Charles de Gaulle circled the desk and shook Mother's hand heartily.

"I have been told so much of both your bravery," he said. "Thank you for granting me the honor of meeting you in the flesh."

"Happy to oblige," said Mother, obviously unimpressed by the general's famed charm. "This is my son, Henri Martin, and his—*our* dog, Brigette."

"Ah yes, I have heard," said General de Gaulle. He turned to Henri and shook his hand, then crouched and scratched Bri around the face and neck. "The young man who crossed many kilometers and avoided capture by the enemy. His childhood dog, who escaped the clutches of the Nazis and defected to rejoin her young master. It is like a storybook, no?"

"They certainly surprised us all," said Mother, beaming at Henri.

"Well, Madame Martin, with Paris finally free from the enemy, I want to congratulate its liberators," said General de Gaulle, standing. "If it would be all right with you, I would like to make you an Officer of the Legion d'Honneur."

Henri couldn't help but gasp. His mother blinked a few times, obviously surprised. The Legion of Honor was France's highest military order, and only the most celebrated soldiers and freedom fighters were given such an opportunity.

"Thank you, General," said Mother, sounding, Henri thought, a little kinder than she had when she'd first entered.

"Monsieur Martin, I wish I could bestow the same honor upon you, and upon Brigette," said General de Gaulle, "but alas, you are too young, and she is a dog. Such is life, eh? What I can tell you is that France is eternally grateful for your hard work. We could not have made it out of this war without you."

"*Merci*, General," said Henri. Then, to Bri, "Hear that, girl? We're heroes!" Brigette barked excitedly, getting an odd little smile from the general.

"Well, unless there's anything else, we'll be on our way," said Mother. "My son would like to take part in some of the celebrations going on today."

"Please," said the general. "Only be careful, that journalist Hemingway is lurking around the city today, and he'll talk your ear off."

Outside of the palais, the city was one huge party. People embraced and kissed in public. Out of every window, excited Parisians tossed confetti. American, British, and Canadian soldiers were in the streets, some marching proudly, others stopping to say hello to hordes of cheering girls. The boats on the Seine River were honking at waving pedestrians and flew banners reading VIVE LA FRANCE. The air was full of good smells, greetings, and something Henri hadn't heard for a long time—laughter. All around was a sense of freedom, excitement, and hope. They had done it. Paris had been saved from the iron grip of Hitler and his legion of death.

But Henri wasn't interested in all that—he had something else in mind. He scanned the crowds at the base of the palais steps, trying to pick out one soldier in particular.

"They might have forgotten," said Linda,

seeing her son's eyes wander. "I'm sorry, Henri, it's just a busy day—"

"THERE he is!" Henri turned as a crew of soldiers came up the steps of the palais. At the head of them was Jake Tanaka. On his shoulders sat Elle, looking almost unrecognizable to Henri in a clean yellow sundress and with a bow in her hair. Hopping by his side was Ace. Ace wore a cast on his one leg, but he still managed to leap around excitedly.

Jake let Elle down, and she first hugged Henri, then shook Linda's hand. Henri knelt down to pet Ace, who gave his face and neck a round of licks. Jake tossed Bri one of his gross treats, which she nimbly caught in midair.

"Careful, she's getting addicted to those things," said Henri.

"Ah, she'll be fine," said Elle in her accented English. "A snack now and then never hurt nobody. Ain't that right, Bri?"

"Your English is getting good," said Henri, "but you sound like a soldier. People don't talk like that in the real world, even in America."

"Nah," she said. "From what I hear, Cleveland is, how do you say, the tough town. I must be ready."

"How was your official meeting?" asked Jake, nodding to the palais.

"It was interesting," said Mother, smiling despite herself. "De Gaulle certainly thinks he's more charismatic than he is. How long are you in staying in Paris?"

"Ah, just for the party today, and then we're heading back," said Jake. "This little guy is getting honorably discharged for getting injured in battle. They're going to send him to his forever home in Ohio. Thankfully, he won't go it alone." He ruffled the little girl's hair, and she giggled.

"That's good," said Henri. He'd been happy when he heard that Ace's owners had offered to adopt Elle. It wasn't common for American families to do such things—especially during wartime—but Ace had grown so attached to her that they just couldn't say no. Henri was sad that he'd never see her again . . . but then again, their journey together had taught him that life was full of surprises. Who knew? Maybe after the war he'd take a trip to Cleveland. Anything was possible!

Henri gave Ace a little hug and laughed as the dog licked his ear. Then he stood, found the envelope in his pocket, and handed it to Jake. "This is a letter I wrote for Ace's owners and Elle's new parents. It tells them just how brave he was and how much he helped me. Can you make sure they get it?"

"Of course," said Jake, taking the letter. "I know I keep saying this, kid, but thank you so much. Ace would still be in that tree if it wasn't for you. I'll tell his family that too." He clapped Henri on the shoulder, then looked to Ace and Elle. "All right, troops, we better get a move on. Thanks again, kid. If you're ever in California, let me know."

Elle ran to Henri and gave him one final tight hug.

"Thanks for the coat," she said.

"Thanks for saving my life," he said.

Jake, Elle, and Ace headed off into the crowds of parties. One by one, the other soldiers in Jake's crew came over and shook Henri's hand or gave him a slap on the shoulders. Then they, too, disappeared into the noise and excitement of the city.

"Can we go watch some of the parade?" asked Henri.

Mother looked exhausted even thinking about it. She ruffled Henri's hair. "I'm a little tired, sweetheart. It's been a long week . . . and month. I might just head home."

"Can Brigette and I go, then?" asked Henri.

For a moment Mother looked unsure, as though letting Henri go meant she might never see him again . . . but then she smiled and nodded. "Very well. I think you've earned it, my little soldier. Just be home by four. I love you."

"Love you too," he said, and gave Mother a hug. Then Henri ran off into the crowds, Brigette barking happily at his side, both of them filled with hope and excitement knowing what they'd done, all they'd lost and regained.

Ace walked Elle out to the car. The little girl stooped to scratch his head for the fourth time, and once again, Ace let her. He could hear by the beating of her heart that she was nervous. He wanted to comfort her in any way he could. After all, he couldn't blame her. From what Ace could gather, this was her first time in an airplane. He remembered how scared he'd been on his first training flight—*and* how scared he'd been during the mission.

There was no shame in being a little frightened of a new experience.

Or a little sad, Ace thought, about saying goodbye.

Jake waited in the street for them, holding open the car door. He smiled warmly at Elle and gave her a big last hug before putting her in the backseat. It warmed Ace's heart to watch them together. Since he'd rescued her, Jake had treated Elle like his own pup.

Jake looked down at Ace. Ace whimpered without planning to. After all this time, after everything they'd been through, their mission together was at an end. He could see that he wasn't the only one feeling down about it—Jake's eyes were wet, and his smile was pulled tight at the edges.

He was a fine human, Jake was. Ace would

miss him terribly.

Jake leaned down to pick him up . . . but just for old time's sake, Ace jumped out of the way and barked. When Jake put his hands on his hips and said, "*Aaace* . . ." he jumped up on his hind legs and waved his front paws in the air. Jake laughed and bent down again. This time, Ace let himself be picked up, and let his human friend give him one final hug before putting him in the car with Elle.

"Good boy, Ace," said Jake before closing the car door.

Ace watched him through the back window as they sped away.

Good boy, Jake, thought Ace.

As the car drove off into the future, Ace put his head down on Elle's lap and let her pet his back. He had a long journey ahead of him, he knew, but it would be worth it. Elle was a sweetheart, and she would take good care of him. And she would fit in well with the Cleveland family. Ma and Pop would treat her right, and Reggie would be a good older brother. They would be happy together.

His eyes began to drift closed . . .

When the smell hit him.

Ace sat up and went to the window. It had only been a shred of scent, but it had been enough. Perhaps he'd imagined it—

No. There, in the alley. It was only a glimpse, a blur of sharp black, but it was enough.

So they hadn't caught her after all.

Krieger stood in the shadows, watching him. For the brief instant they saw each other, Ace could sense the anger behind her gaze. She was a street dog now, living in a free city, with no masters of her own . . . but that hate had become a part of her. And she hated no one more than Ace, the dog who escaped her clutches.

Ace growled. He should jump out of the car and go after her. He should tell Elle or Jake that she was still out there. He should let them all know that she'd somehow stayed alive—

"Ace?"

Ace looked back at Elle. Her sweet face looked surprised and a little scared.

No.

Ace laid back down and put his head on her lap.

Yes, Krieger was still out there—but so was

the enemy, in some form or another. A boy would be cruel to Reggie. A master would kick at Ace on the street. A neighbor would threaten to call the pound on him. There would always be evil and anger out there, waiting to bite you if you weren't careful.

But there was also kindness, and hope. For every enemy shadow, there was a good person. Like Henri, the boy who saved him out on those wet, rainy hills that fateful night when everything changed. Like Jake, who had trained him, taught him, and taken him on the mission. And like Elle, this sweet girl who now ran her hand across his fur and whispered, "Good boy, Ace."

Ace had a new mission now. He'd return to the family and look after this little girl pup. And if evil ever came looking for them, Ace would be ready. He would protect them. That's what good soldiers did.

BATTLE FACTS

The invasion of Normandy, France, was one of the most important turning points of World War II. Here are a few things you should know about it:

Q. What lead up to the invasion of Normandy?
A. By 1944, World War II had been going full force for some time, and the world was growing weary. Nazi Germany, led by racist dictator Adolf Hitler, had invaded Poland, Denmark, Norway, Belgium, the Netherlands, and Northern France. The Nazis had begun rounding up everyone they considered inferior to Hitler's "master race" ideal—specifically Europe's Jews, homosexuals, and people of color—and sending them to concentration camps.

The British, Canadians, and Americans had fought against Germany as well as its allies Italy and Japan, but resources were running low. London was in shambles after considerable bombing

by the Germans, and both America and Great Britain were suffering from shortages of food, metal, and rubber.

Q. How did the invasion of Normandy occur?
A. The area of coastal France called Normandy was invaded by British, Canadian, and American troops in the single largest amphibious assault in recorded history.

The invasion began in the early morning of June 6, 1944, with paratroopers dropping into Northern France along the English Channel. Then Operation Neptune (named after the Roman god of the sea) began, in which ships carrying Allied troops landed on the beaches along Normandy and attacked German troops stationed there.

All of this was part of Operation Overlord, the grand Allied plan to reclaim Western Europe. This plan would take longer than just one day of battle, but the beach invasions of Operation Neptune were the first step to reclaiming Europe from the Nazis.

INVASION STATS

Date: June 6, 1944.

Original dates: May 1 and June 4, but delayed by weather on both counts.

Length of Normandy coast invaded: 60 miles.

Sea invasion: 4,126 amphibious assault craft.

Air invasion: 11,000 aircraft.

Allied troops invading France: Approximately 156,000.

Paratroopers: 13,000.

Countries involved in invasion: United States, Great Britain, and Canada.

Beaches landed: Five, codenamed Omaha, Utah, Gold, Sword, and Juno.

Q. Where did the term "D-Day" come from?
A. "D-Day" is a military term used to refer to a day on which an armored battle is taking place. While the invasion of Normandy has become synonymous with the term, it is not technically the only D-Day in military history.

The "D" in D-Day has been given several

meanings—due to the loss of life and chaos that often come with battle, many believe "D-Day" is a shortening for "Doomsday," which means the end of the world—but the most commonly held one today is that it also means "Day," so D-Day is a shortened version of "the Day of All Days."

DEPICTIONS OF D-DAY

Because of its military importance and the intensity of the battle, it has been depicted in various pieces of media. Here are some of the most famous:

The Longest Day (film, 1962): This classic Hollywood war film shows an idealized depiction of the D-Day invasion, and it is famous for performances from classic actors like John Wayne, Robert Mitchum, and Richard Burton.

Saving Private Ryan (film, 1998): Steven Spielberg's epic World War II film opens with a realistic depiction of the invasion of Omaha Beach.

Sabaton, *Primo Victoria* (album, 2005): Swedish heavy metal band Sabaton wrote an entire album about World War II, and its opening track, "Primo Victoria," is a rollicking battle cry describing of the events of Operation Overlord.

Q. How did the invasion of Normandy change the course of the war?

A. D-Day gave the Allies entrance into France so they could continue bringing in soldiers, weaponry, and infrastructure. It also gave the Allies a fresh understanding of German military tactics. Many people believe that the high level of German bureaucracy and their focus on the ethnic cleansing of Europe allowed for their defeat at Normandy.

More important, D-Day changed public morale about the war. For many, the Nazis had an invincible stranglehold on Europe, and the fear that they might invade North America was very real. D-Day showed the world that the Nazis could be beaten, that Europe could be invaded, and that the tide of the war might finally be changing.

December 7, 1941—
Attack on Pearl Harbor

December 8, 1941—
US enters the war

September 1, 1939—
Germany invades Poland;
war breaks out in Europe

1939 **1940** **1941** **1942**

September 1940—
US government
begins the draft

January 1942—
Dogs for Defense
program is founded

July 1942—
US government
commits to use of
trained war dogs

August 1942—
US begins work on
atomic bomb

WORLD WAR II

May 7, 1945—
German forces surrender

May 8, 1945—
V-E Day (Victory in Europe)

September 1943—
Italian forces
surrender

August 6, 1945—
Atomic bomb dropped on Hiroshima

August 9, 1945—
Atomic bomb dropped on Nagasaki

August 14, 1945—
Japanese forces surrender

September 2, 1945—
V-J Day (Victory in Japan),
Japanese sign surrender

1943

1944

1945

April 22, 1944—
Allied forces begin
practicing for the invasion

May, 1944—
Troops all over Britain
move to staging areas

August 25, 1944—
Paris is freed from
German control

June 4, 1944—
Original D-Day date, cancelled
by General Eisenhower because
of poor weather

June 5, 1944—
Eisenhower approves
invasion

June 6, 1944—
D-Day at Normandy in
France

TIMELINE

The first of nearly 1,200 aircraft take off from England

Allied paratroopers sighted by German forces

American forces land on Omaha Beach

12:11 AM	1:50 AM	1:55 AM	5:58 AM	6:30 AM	7:25 AM

Sunrise

German admiral sends word to Berlin that the Allies are invading

British and Free French forces land at Sword Beach

OF D-DAY

On Omaha Beach, Americans take their first four German prisoners

Allies liberate Bayeux, the first French city to be freed following the invasion

British forces land at Gold Beach

| 7:35 AM | 7:55 AM | 8:35 AM | 10:30 AM | JUNE 7 |

British and Canadian forces land at Juno Beach

American paratroopers from Dog Company fight near Utah Beach

Fighting continues through the afternoon and night

Q. Were the characters in this story real?

A. Some of the historical figures in this book *were* real people. Henri Tardivat was a celebrated French freedom fighter, and General Charles de Gaulle was a French politician who helped defeat the Nazis (though he later became a controversial figure in French history). Henri and his mother, Linda, are not real, but Linda was based on an actual freedom fighter named Nancy Wake.

Q. Who was Nancy Wake?

A. Nancy Wake, aka the White Mouse, was a secret agent and freedom fighter in France during World War II. She was born in New Zealand but spent most of her childhood in Australia. She became a journalist in New York and London and married a French industrialist in Paris. There, she saw the Nazis rise to power and take over France. She became a pivotal part of the French Resistance, and by 1943 she was the Nazis' most-wanted person, with a five-million-franc bounty on her head—approximately $6,700,000 today!

Wake was famous for both her beauty and her bravery. One minute, she was flirting with

German guards to get past checkpoints with secret documents, the next she was leading armed assaults with teams of freedom fighters at her disposal. Wake was instrumental in fighting sexism during the war, proving that women were just as capable and powerful on the battlefield and behind enemy lines as they were in the mess hall or the infirmary.

Q. Did dogs actually parachute into war?
A. Yes! The British military really did have dogs on the planes that flew into Normandy at D-Day. These "paradogs" were trained to jump out of planes wearing parachutes. When they landed, they would search for booby traps and tripwires, suss out groups of enemy soldiers, and find escape routes for the soldiers they were working with. They were also big morale boosters for soldiers who felt a little run down by a long war!

Many paradogs were actually household dogs who were donated to the army and trained to be soldiers and paratroopers. Because of food shortages caused by the war, many British households couldn't afford to feed themselves AND their

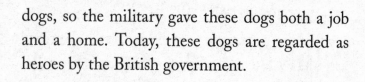

dogs, so the military gave these dogs both a job and a home. Today, these dogs are regarded as heroes by the British government.

Q. Who was a famous paradog?

A. One specific paradog of some note was Bing, an Alsatian-collie mix who parachuted into Normandy during the D-Day invasion. Like Ace, Bing was a great paradog in practice, but on D-Day itself, she got scared by the gunfire and had to be thrown out of the plane. Like Ace, she was later found dangling from a tree, having suffered injuries in her landing. However, she proved invaluable to soldiers by helping them sniff out traps and find provisions in enemy territory. Bing is considered a hero by the British government.

BRIAN AKA BING
PARACHUTE BATTALION HERO DOG

NATIONALITY: BRITISH

BREED: ALSATIAN-COLLIE MIX

JOB: PARATROOPER

STRENGTHS: BRAVERY, ALERTNESS, LOYALTY

TRAINING: WAR DOG TRAINING SCHOOL

STATIONED: EUROPEAN FRONT

HEROIC MOMENT: SAVING TROOPS FROM TRAPS IN FRANCE DURING D-DAY

HONORS: PDSA DICKIN MEDAL, BRITAIN'S HIGHEST HONOR FOR DOGS

STUBBY

NATIONALITY: AMERICAN

BREED: UNKNOWN

JOB: 102ND INFANTRY DIVISION MASCOT

STRENGTHS: DETERMINATION, BRAVERY, CLEVERNESS

TRAINING: YALE UNIVERSITY

STATIONED: FRANCE

HEROIC MOMENT: CAPTURING A GERMAN SPY WHO WAS TRYING TO MAP ALLIED TRENCHES

HONORS: HUMANE SOCIETY GOLD MEDAL, WOUND STRIPE FOR BEING INJURED IN THE LINE OF DUTY

FRENCH AND GERMAN WORDS AND TERMS

Since this story is set in France and involves German soldiers, both the French and German languages come regularly into play. Here are some translations of the terms we use in this book, as well as how to say them.

French:

monsieur (miss-YOU): Mister.

vive la France (VEE-vuh lah Fronss): "Long live France." This was a common slogan for French Resistance fighters during the war.

mon Dieu (mohn DYOO): My God.

renard (reh-NAHRD): Fox.

blanc (blonk): White.

voilà (vwa-LA): There it is! (the French version of "Tada!")

merci (mehr-SEE): Thank you.

German:

guten Tag (GOO-ten TOGG): Good day/good morning.

Krieg (creeg): War.

Krieger (CREE-gerr): Warrior.

Hund (hoond): Dog.

Blitz: Lightning.

Stielhandgranate (SHTEEL-hand-greh-NOT): Stick hand grenade. Specifically, a form of hand grenade used heavily by Germany in World War II.

Tollpatsch (TOLL-pach): Klutz, oaf, or clumsy person.

mein Freund (mine frOYnd): My friend.

Führer (FYOO-rerr): Leader. A term commonly used by Nazis to refer to Adolf Hitler.

Join the Fight!

DON'T MISS THE FIRST
ACTION—PACKED MISSION

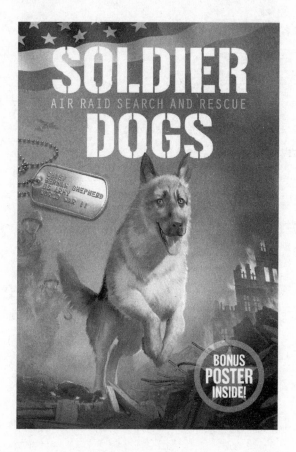

CHAPTER 1

JUNE 1, 1942
2:33 A.M.
CANTERBURY, ENGLAND

Twelve-year-old Matt Dawson hunched in the darkness as bombs fell outside the half-collapsed movie theater. He hugged his knees in the cramped space beneath a fallen balcony. His breath came loud and panicked. He was trapped.

He could hear his ten-year-old foster sister, Rachel, trying to stifle her crying nearby, but he couldn't see her. Rubble surrounded them both. There was no way out. Sweat pricked Matt's skin, and the air was clogged with smoke and dust.

He heard the shriek of air-raid sirens and the

groan of a wall collapsing. How long before the rubble fell on him and his sister?

He wanted to give up, but he needed to be brave for Rachel, just like his brother, Eric, used to be brave for him. He didn't feel brave, though. All he felt was scared. Still, he stretched his arm through the rubble until his fingertips barely touched Rachel's.

"It's going to be okay," he told her, but he didn't really believe it.

Matt was American. His parents had brought him to England so his father could help with the war effort. Then the entire family had moved to Canterbury to escape the air raids in London. But the raids had changed targets, and now he and Rachel were trapped inside a ruined movie theater and the bombs were still falling.

Nobody could find them. Nobody could save them.

"Do you think the raid is over?" Rachel whispered into the darkness.

"Maybe. Or maybe there are more waves coming."

"There can't be! When will it stop? When will— Oh!"

"What?"

"I think I heard people!" Rachel took a breath. "Help! Help!"

"We're in the movie theater!" Matt yelled, even though he didn't hear anyone. "We're trapped!"

He heard a shout from the street, muffled by the rubble. A bunch of voices that sounded like firemen, desperately battling a blaze. Firemen like his brother, Eric.

"Help!" Matt yelled. "We're trapped!"

"There's nobody in the movie theater," a man's voice said.

"Are you sure?" another voice asked.

"In here!" Matt called. "Hello?"

"We're trapped!" Rachel shouted, in her accented voice. "Help!"

The men couldn't hear them through the rubble. Not with the sirens screaming and the fires roaring.

"It's all clear," the first man said. "Move out."

"No!" Matt shouted. "WE'RE IN HERE!"

The voices faded away . . . then Matt heard a distant barking.

"Chief!" Matt shouted. "Chief!"

Chief's barking grew more urgent.

"Chief!" Rachel yelled.

"What is that mutt doing?" the first man said. "We've got a situation around the corner. Get a wiggle on!"

"Drag him along," the second man said, when the barks became sharper. "There's nobody in the theater. The mangy fleabag just wants to watch a movie . . ."

Matt and Rachel screamed and shouted, but the voices grew fainter and fainter.

Until they disappeared—even Chief's.

And Matt and Rachel were alone. Again.

Read them all!

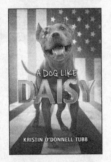